Also by Steven Key Meyers

Fiction

My Hollywood Memoir and Other Fiction
(plus *Sidestep, Big Luck* and *Save the Max Man!)*

That's My Story
(plus *The Last Posse)*

Family Romance

My Mad Russian: Three Tales
(plus *Another's Fool* and *I Remember Caramoor)*

The Wedding on Big Bone Hill
(plus *Junkie, Indiana)*

Springtime in Siena
(plus *The Man Who Owned New York)*

All That Money

Good People

Nonfiction

The Man in the Balloon:
Harvey Joiner's Wondrous 1877

Plays

A Journal of the Plague Year,
and Other Plays and Adaptations

QUEER'S *PROGRESS*

A Novel

Steven Key Meyers

Queer's Progress

ISBN 978-1-7330465-3-4

All characters appearing in this work are fictitious. Any resemblance to real persons, living or dead, is coincidental.

Revised edition 2023

SMASH
&GRAB
PRESS

for my mother and father

But for you, too, Frank and Albert. You taught me a lot, for which I'm grateful. Rest in peace.

Queer's Progress

SHE HAD WATCHED life, since she came to London, with a sort of despair—motivated and busy, always, always progressing; even people pausing on bridges seemed to pause with a purpose; no bird seemed to pursue a quite aimless flight. The spring of the works seemed unfound only by her. . . .

Elizabeth Bowen
The Death of the Heart

NOW I BEGIN to reap the benefits of my hazards.

John Bunyan
Pilgrim's Progress

Chapters

1. *Cutest Geek I Ever Saw*

MY FAMILY'S fucked up beyond the norm, OK? That's why I work like a maniac, to keep out of the house. Not that it helps when everyone I meet is so fucked up.

But even when I try to stay busy, things can slow up around me, trap me in syrup. Tuesday afternoon, nothing's going on, except the sun's pouring down hot honey, making people shift in their seats. Stays over the roof till late, but once it starts rolling for Jersey, even in wintertime they have to get out from under, move to the shade wedged beneath the high west windows. *Flee.*

So I'm standing in the cage thinking, *What now? What next?* This is 1991, January—the week after we start bombing Iraq. That first night they close the exits, just to get *out* of the 42nd Street Library everyone—even *us*—has to go through the front, no explanation, descend the marble staircases beneath the giant vaults with the sinking sensation of *What'd I do?* In the Great Hall guards want to see every scrap of paper.

But it's *war. Cool,* actually.

"You OK, Eddie?" goes Akesha.

"Fine," I snap. Poor Akesha. But she knows I have my moods.

The dumbwaiter chucks into place and I take out a load of books, punch in the numbers, spread them along the counter. Usually that causes a stir, people race up to get theirs. But no one moves. Which means the sun's washing out the lightboard.

"Eddie?" says Akesha.

"What?"

She goes off to tell her troubles to one of the girls. Everyone's fidgeting like ants under a magnifying glass. Nothing to do but watch. It amuses me. These are people who choose a chair in the morning like they're moving in for good—size up the neighbors, lay out their pads and pens (counting every one), pull the next chair closer and drape their coat over it. *Oy!*

Then through Genealogy's bronze double doors steps an *angel*. Shaggy head gilded by sun, green eyes snapping with thought, he walks through the room straight at *me*. Glances at the board, shows his number card and says, "Four-thirty-four, please," part of the load that's just come up.

"Hi!" I go. Don't know why. Startles a flash behind his specs. Cutest geek I ever saw. Now I recognize him, he's a regular. What have I been missing?

"Hello," he says, wary.

"So what're you working on, anyway?" I ask, shoving over a pile of musty shit. "You always get the oldest stuff."

"On Walter Terse?" he says. "Annotating his diaries?"

"Yeah?" I say enthusiastically, thinking *who?* Which does not get past him.

"The 'Voluble Victorian'? English novelist-slash-essayist?"

"Cool!" I go. Above his red-gold beard his eyes are like jewels.

"Well, he mentions a lot of people and events that don't mean much anymore, so it's my job to try and figure them out so my boss can write footnotes."

"Wow!"

"Thank you," he says, and off he goes.

Flip his number off. A line's forming. Sun comes off the board, people converge.

"On break," I yell down to Alan.

"Eduardo, you can't just– Eduardo, come back here!"

Out of the cage, past the lascivious stare of the librarian on duty (what law is it says they have to be gay?), down the blazing shelves to the *Dictionary of National Biography*. Three fucking pages on "Walter Ivanhoe Terse (1827-1907), prolific novelist and social reformer fondly remembered as the *Voluble Victorian*." Very interesting.

Back to the cage. The line now epic in length. Snakes past the Bibles, where the regulars hunting lottery numbers curse the ones on line. Start working through the backlog. The girls never keep up, and Alan's hopeless. When things get busy he rises up from his lair to get in our way, though his tie and important expression reassure the ones waiting.

"Did you hear me, Eduardo?"

"I'm back, Alan, don't get your balls in an uproar."

Old line. Still works.

"Downstairs," he says. "*Now*."

OK, down the steep flight to the dark dusty corner where rotting books hide his desk. Mildew's unbelievable.

"Sit down," he says.

"Can't, I'll get asthma."

"Eddie, your shift has *three* breaks, scheduled for—"

Yeah, yeah, we work it out. Boss has to show he's boss. No problem. Stand and wheeze a little, flip him my Goya urchin look and he rushes through it, creases in his forehead underlining his words: "—'cause I don't want to lose you, I know it's only part-time and doesn't pay much, but it's not so bad, really. I mean, *is* it?"

"I like it," I say. "Sorry, Alan, won't happen again." And

upstairs we go. No one gets books to the people faster than I do.

Later I'm giving one to a woman, telling her when the other two arrive we'll light up her number again, give us a few, when I see the Terse guy heading for the return window. Go over to take personal delivery. Actually, I know his name from the call slips: Andrew Thomas. Two first names. Waspy enough, I don't think?

"Thanks," he says, sliding books beneath the bars.

"Find it?" I ask.

"No," he says. Smiles. "That is—"

"Every little bit helps?"

"It adds up."

"Would you agree *The League of Optimists* is Terse's best?"

Smile goes wide for a second. Good teeth. But the eyes go panicky, and *I* feel it, too: Something grabbing at my *crotch?* The *fuck?*

He stumbles towards the catalog room, and someone gooses me, really digs into my ass. "Hey, big boy, Alan says—"

It's Akesha. Downstairs where we hang out there's a Polaroid on the wall, seven of us jamming faces together. Five are girls, and one day I realize I've fucked every one of them. It's embarrassing.

"Oh Akesha, let's go somewhere."

"There's that place," she says. "In the stacks."

"Eduardo!" calls Alan. Nods at the line.

Back to the salt mines.

2. *Cancer*

"NED HAMET, HIS 4:00 o'clock?"

"The doctor will be right with you, Mr. Hamet."

My ghostly outline in her window unnerved me, though it did take the years off. A nurse put me in an examining room. Examining rooms make me nervous—autopsy rooms with padding. I preferred looking down at the ants negotiating First Avenue's slush 20 stories below to sitting on the jointed slab and staring at instruments of torture ranged along the walls. Then I glanced across at the other wing. Amazing what they'll do in a hospital with curtains wide open. Sickmaking.

Dr. Kushner bustled in. Top dermatologist in the city. Have to admire him, rolling up the big bucks healing people. Did I miss my calling?

"How are you, Ned?" Shook my hand and washed his, meaning no insult.

"Hello, Doc," I said. "Oh, the usual: Two moles on my back, plus this thing on my nose."

"Have a seat, lie back."

He meant on the slab. Cranked it flat, pulled down the light, and went out of focus as he came in close on my nose.

A negligible little growth, a freckle or mole like those that turn up on my back as regularly as rocks in spring plowing, all because when I was young no one knew to keep out of the sun. Hardly visible, but they drive me crazy. I know the procedure: Freeze them with that super-thin needle, sluice them off with laser beams or whatever, slap on a Band-Aid, wish me good day and leave it to the receptionist to charge me the outrageous fee ten minutes of the good doctor's time goes for.

Being examined by a doctor's a special kind of ecstasy, like conversing with God or being adored by a lover. I'm a hypochondriac, no denying that, but at least I don't indulge in private hysteria. No, I make the rounds of the leading specialists, and do what they tell me, too: My drinking's strictly medicinal, I shake my booty to music half an hour daily, and a rabbit would envy my diet (but I *insist* on regularity: A bowel movement in the morning takes a load off my mind).

"Hmm," Dr. Kushner said pleasantly. This was a new note; usually he was reassuringly brusque. "Take off your shirt and lie on your tummy, we'll do your back first."

He rendered my back again flawless, but all I could think of—*roaring* in my ears—was the word I cannot say. I can say heart attack—my heart's never given me a moment's concern. I can say AIDS, which I intend never to get. But one word I *cannot* bring myself to utter.

Dr. Kushner had no such compunction. Turned me over and loomed again.

"Looks like a skin cancer, Ned," he said. "Let's take it off, get it biopsied."

"Can—?"

I could go no further. One *horrifying* thought: *Die with my novel unpublished?*

"Probably just basal cell, though it could be squamous cell or malignant mela— Hold *still*. Even if it *is* a bad one, this should take care of it, unless it's already metasta— Hold *still,* dammit!"

Is this what it comes to, a jolly sentence of death over First Avenue?

"Ned, you're in your 60s, you have to expect—"

The worst day of my life darkened.

"Beg pardon, Doc, I don't turn 60 for *months* yet."

"Whatever." *Whatever!* "Hey, this is nothing. Had a patient yesterday, nice young guy, acne into his 30s?"

"Don't think I'd like him," I said.

"Out of here by 4:30, walks down to 14th Street, gets stabbed."

"Oh my God!"

"I mean, it's New York: Jeep comes down the sidewalk, get out of the way, right? But this poor schmuck slaps it as it goes past. Reminding the driver of his manners? Guy gets out with a knife. I mean?"

"Did he die?"

"Course he died," said Dr. Kushner. "What kind of story is it if he doesn't die? Point is, one little skin cancer. And we haven't even biopsied it yet, for goodness sake."

Doctors are too close to death to know what it means. Off he sent me into the world with a Band-Aid across my nose. I felt grotesque. Leprous. Doomed. And on the 23rd Street crosstown bus came the first stab of what I knew was pancreatic cancer, the invariably fatal kind. And with church that evening!

I was going to ask the young man sitting next to me to hold me, just *hold* me, but at Broadway he bounced off the bus.

3. *Expecting*

AFTER WORK CATCH the uptown One at Times Square. By 137th Street I finish another chapter of *Pride and Prejudice* for Nineteenth-Century Novel. Five chapters to go, other homework, too, but the instant I get in Mami says go up to Suriya's.

"Can't, Mami: Homework."

"*Su mama me llamó.*"

"Mami, *no* – "

No arguing with your mother, is there?

Take the stairs, knock. Hear a shuffle towards the door. Opens on the robed figure and haggard face of Suriya, who's none too pretty the best of times. Very few teeth left, and she's not 30. Always had to turn off the lights to do it with her. But great hair – dreads like stuffed animals.

Her mother leans on a doorway, mad as hell. "Lock that door." Bites off the words.

Suriya locks it and puts her arms around me. "Eduardo."

I skip away. "Hey, Suriya, what's up?"

"*See?* She got news for you, big man. Take it like a man." Can't tell if she's fucked up or not. Always smells like crack up there.

"Eduardo," Suriya manages. Puts hands to her eyes and snuffles.

"Suriya, I got to go finish *Pride and Prejudice* – "

"Big man!" mama repeats.

"Eduardo, I'm late."

Fuck.

"We gon' have a beautiful little baby."

"And you gon' marry her!" says Mama, charging over. "You play the game, you do the time! She too good for you – "

And on and on. I smile and nod and reassure Suriya, saying it's all right, we'll have such fun, I love kids, always wanted a son, we can do it tomorrow in Atlantic City if she wants, I'll quit school and maybe her cousin can find a place for me, even a corner of my own, if so we'll buy a Range Rover, red if she insists, though I prefer white.

She wants to fuck, but I tell her she has to take care of herself. Kiss her on the eyelids, temples, the backs of her hands, her fingertips, brush her lips lightly, give mama a bear hug and a smackeroo and, making no fast moves, leave. Even wait for the elevator so she has extra time to hang from her door admiring me.

Downstairs I luck out. José, Mami's boyfriend, is home but off on troubles of his own, like maybe he lost his job again. He does maintenance work Midtown. Turns bloodshot eyes on me, but I know she didn't tell him anything.

In my room I put on extra underwear, two extra shirts and my coat, load up my backpack with school stuff, head for the door.

"¿Eduardo?" says Mami.

"Where the fuck–?" goes José.

Last I hear. Race down the steps, past the guys getting high in the lobby–usually I hang, so they overlook it–and call Jaime collect from around the corner.

He's not happy, but what's he going to say, No, he's fresh out of *floors?* We're brothers. Closer, even–friends since 3rd grade. So I wait on the subway steps and when the One rolls in, run down, do a stunt over the turnstile and jump on. Don't have a token or any money, either.

Getting to East Harlem's a bitch and I'm beat when I get there, but Jaime's glad to see me, actually. Things are going good. He's hooked up with our godmother Tia Luisa and is starting to get someplace. In New York if you tell someone it fell off the truck, their eyes light up. Won't pay retail, but they'll buy stuff they wouldn't otherwise. I mean, when the label says Calvin Klein, you love the way it looks, right?

So by the time I fall asleep, happy Elizabeth Bennett's landed her rich boyfriend at last, my wardrobe's been augmented by Calvin Klein underwear and a Ralph Lauren Polo shirt that might be real and a YSL scarf.

The scarf is for fags, though.

4. *REWARDING PROPOSITION*

I WAS A *SAINT* to show up at church that night. But why stay home to brood about my impending demise when I could do that anywhere?

Besides, when I called over to Gramercy Park to see if I had an 8:00 o'clock, Harry told me the Andrew he'd just scheduled sounded like a coming-outer.

While I waited for Harry's 7:00 o'clock to finish, there came a ruckus from someone struggling with the street door. Went down and let in a supremely nervous young man.

"Thank you," he said, and bounded up the steps and turned around twice before beseeching me, "Do you know where Gays Reaching Out—?"

"*I'm* GRO," I told him. "Have a seat, Andrew."

It staggered him. He looked cornered. Found out. Went white. *Oh, yes,* I said to myself: *Coming-outer.*

"I'm Ned." He groped for my hand like a drowning man for his straw. "They're still in our room. Be a minute yet."

Sitting down, he refused my offer of a mint, but asked, "What is this church? Episcopalian?"

"*Mais oui.* They give us the space. How did you find out about GRO?"

"Signboard? 'Gays Reaching Out—free peer counseling'?"

I nodded. Apparently there's an appeal to coming out under institutional auspices. Once Harry and his counselee left, I ushered Andrew into our little room of soiled tan paint, battered wooden desk, plastic chair and vinyl couch.

"I'll be settled in about two minutes," I said, looking for a pen that worked and observing him.

Virgin of 26, I guessed, wearing under his winter coat what could be his father's clothes (particularly if Dad bought his pants by mail) and hiding his own advantages with an odd haircut, a beard, black-framed glasses. Even so, I found his face forgivable. The glasses made his eyes small – glasses can seal off an entire personality – but they had a quality anyway. Homosexually virgin, I mean; thought he might well be married. Could picture his intellectual wife.

Put my cigarettes and matches on the desk, opened the notebook, read aloud, "Kevin ten dollars" and looked in the cash box.

"Oh!" said Andrew, and handed me a $10 bill. "Here."

Made a notation and asked, "Mind if I smoke?"

"No."

Did the best Paul Henreid you can lighting up a single cigarette while sporting a Band-Aid across your nose. Filled my lungs and, looking upwards, breathed out slowly. I do smoke well. Always have.

Meanwhile Andrew shook like a murderer on the verge of confessing.

I asked, "Are you a minister?"

"No," he said, *fear* in the voice. "No, I'm not a minister."

Took another drag. We had an hour.

"Why would you ask that? I don't even believe in God."

"Is that a prerequisite? No, your appearance, your manner, your speech. Were you raised in a religion?"

"Roman Catholic."

"It fits," I noted. "Oh, how it fits! Are you married?"

"No, I'm not married."

Took another drag. A man coming out at 40 or 50 has its sad side, though I'll do what I can, but Andrew was young – frankly a more rewarding proposition for a counselor.

"Harry didn't write down any specifics," I hinted.

"Well," said Andrew. "Well, today I met—or didn't *meet*—but we spoke—but it's like looking through glass. . . Well, here's the thing: I'm gay, I know it, but I have no sexual life, and don't know how to start one."

Said it and lived.

"I must have missed school the day everybody else got clued in."

Like dynamiting a dam. Always is. Talked nonstop for 40 minutes. Distant father, fairweather mother—two of those suburban parents who find support in their own rigidity. Hated sports, never liked dating girls. In New York a year, sentenced to solitary confinement—nodding acquaintances, no friends. Lonely and unhappy, thoughts of suicide. Just that day he'd walked the length of the New York Public Library's reading room, eyes glued to the denim glow of a page's crotch, and panicked—*ran*—when the kid actually *spoke* to him!

"How long have you known?"

"Since I was—three?" he said.

"Isn't it amazing?" I remarked. "Children aren't even *thinking* about sex, but gay kids feel branded from birth. I *hoped* things were getting easier for you young folks."

His job did interest me. Library research takes a knack I respect, and I'd looked with interest into the first published volumes of Terse's diaries. I even like his clumsy novels, for Terse wrote about the world he lived in, not the Never-Neverland of his day that preceded the Hollywoodland of ours as fiction's usual setting.

"Why aren't you teaching?" I asked.

"I like what I'm doing."

"Are you a private scholar?" Meaning rich.

"No, no, but the Terse Project's funded by the NEH, foundations, all that. I'm full-time, and Professor Onorato also has a full-time editor plus a crew of student research assistants."

"I see."

Not entirely virgin, but he called his few episodes "squalid": a guy in the woods once, another during junior year abroad, and–

"This is hard to say."

"Take your time." Smoke wreathed leisurely ceilingwards.

"I live way over on East 10th past Avenue B–Alphabet City? Loisaida? Across the airshaft's a guy who's always naked. Vacuums naked, scrubs floors naked. With the curtains open."

"Every building has one," I noted.

"Well. I'm ashamed to say this."

"You gave him back his own medicine?"

He blinked. "Yes."

"Did you get together?"

"Uh-huh."

"How was it?"

"Next day he sealed his windows in plastic."

I had to laugh.

"Slip him our number. He's got bigger problems than you do."

"That page at the Library who spoke to me today? Guess that's why I'm here. He's really cute."

"But is he *gay?*"

"I don't know. The girls certainly like him."

"Andrew, Andrew, Andrew: You don't want straight men, not when you've come out to yourself."

"I don't think he's straight. I have a feeling."

"He's white?"

"Maybe Hispanic?"

"Then he comes from a world different from any you know, and you shouldn't read *anything* into what he might do or say."

"I won't," he said solemnly. "Ned, may I ask how old you are?"

"Twenty-three and a half. I run this little operation. First session's to figure out who should counsel you. In your case I think *I'm* the right one. If you agree—" He nodded. "Then if next Tuesday at 8:00's good—"

"One thing," he said in a suddenly strained voice.

A silence asserted itself. Bit of a surprise. Usually by now they're making me dictate a list of cruise bars. Sexuality long repressed tends to explode.

Popped a mint. Felt quite curious.

"This guy through the airshaft. I have a thing on my testicles. I think it's a chancre."

"Pronounced *chancre*. When did you go to bed with him?"

"Last August."

"*August?* And you wait until *January*—? Give me a look."

Locked the door and he stood up, undid his pants and pulled down his briefs. They always come in horny and seductive, but I swear *this* was a new one on me.

No record-breaker, but definitely nice, and it wasn't no chancre. "That's like a *mole*, you'll have it the rest of your *life*, it's *nothing*."

Endless relief and gratitude as he zipped up. A knock at the door, and I unlocked it to my 9:00 o'clock regular, Billy. One glance at Andrew and— Billy's problem is they all look like gods.

"Next week then?"

"Yes," said Andrew. "Yes, Ned, and thank you!"

Left considerably more chipper than when he arrived.

As the door closed, Billy said, "I'm in love!"

"He's a coming-outer, Billy. He needs a lot of help."

"Oh shit," said that rotten Billy, rolling his eyes. "I know what *that* means."

5. *Not Your Job*

One day at the Library, Andy-Tommy comes up like I'm his new best friend, something different about him I can't put my finger on, flashes his number card and, with this shy smile like he knows something I don't, goes, "Hello, how *are* you?"

"Eddie," says Madeline behind me.

Shove two books across. Head aside: "Hold on." Head forward: "Sir, keep your card for when your last book comes up."

Can't he see her? A *girl* standing two steps away? Turning it over?

"Know that guy, Eddie?" she goes after he walks off looking like I hit him. "See how he looked at you?"

"Madeline, trying to get the books out here," I tell her. So she starts helping, but frozen-faced. Women.

Eventually Andy-Tommy's back, flashing his card again and pressing his lips together like he's some kind of Nordic god, unhappy the lightboard's moved through all the numbers without his last book coming up.

It's an accident, swear to God, but fuck if I'm going to say so. His books come up in one stack: two thick ones on the bottom, slips hanging out, on top two small matched volumes with one slip. Reaching in to get them, the friction of my wrist pulls the top slip out and it sails down the side of the shaft. That *never* happens. But I'm not going to try fishing it out, am I? Stick my fingers into cables and gears? I don't *think* so! Without call slips, we can't give books out, so I send the matched pair back down.

Besides, technically he asked for four books when the limit's three. We have rules, you know.

So he stands there pissed. Do I feel better, even if it was accidental? *Hell,* yes!

They finally send the books back up with his new call slip stapled to the telltale orange of a trace card.

Alan knows, don't ask me how.

"Have a seat, Eduardo."

"Can't, my asthma."

"Eduardo, it's not your job to cause problems around here."

"No," I reply humbly, "we leave that to you."

Guy has a temper. Interesting. Librarians go around butter-wouldn't-melt, sweetly helping you find George Washington's middle name or whatever, but *underneath!* Don't see what they get out of it. I say, got an attitude problem, show it and be proud.

"Eduardo, we both know that you lost those books – "

"Did not."

"Let me put it this way – "

Yak yak yak. We work it out. Not losing my job because of some faggot. A warning.

The rest of my shift, I admit I slam books around some. Once I turn around and catch Akesha and Madeline raising their eyebrows at each other in that way women find so witty.

"Guy came on to me," I tell them.

"Get used to it," advises Madeline.

"They're all that way," says Akesha.

6. *Real Progress*

"Benign?" I asked when Dr. Kushner came on the line.

"No, it was basal cell cancer," he said. "But no big deal. Get another and we'll take *it* off, too, OK. . . ? *OK?"*

My nerveless hands dropped the phone. Who knows how long he spoke into the empty air?

But life goes on. My incision healed, that hateful Band-Aid came off and I had every reason to think I was in remission.

And by our second session, I was making real progress with Andy. He sweetly said talking to me was *solving* his problems, not papering them over. I complimented his perceptiveness. He declared that since meeting me he felt airborne, as after flinging off his backpack on a hiking trip; too poetic for me. Meanwhile, Doldrums, my Skye terrier, humped his leg nonstop.

"By the way, do you like Harry?" I asked. As before, Harry had vacated the room for us. Dolly growls at that black beard, but he's a good man, if not my type.

"He seems nice."

"Do you find him attractive?"

"I wasn't thinking in those terms."

"He likes *you*. Poor man just turned 40."

"What's tragic about that?"

"Oh Andy, in the gay community— We're great at so many things, so tolerant, until it comes to *age*. Where we're the *worst*. Already two friends of mine have killed themselves because they got old."

"That seems. . ."

"Yes?"

"Stupid."

"You're 26? Be 30 soon enough."

"And 40, 50, *90*—I hope. Hope I live to tell the tale."

"You warm an old man's heart."

I explained that before he could be set on the prowl by himself he needed a certain acclimatizing to the gay world—a certain *hardening*—and mentioned various LGBT churches that might be about his speed.

"Especially the Congregation of the Loving Arms of Jesus—"

"'The Loving Arms'? Sounds like a gay pub."

"They have *coffee* hours, Andy: Easiest way in the world to meet people."

Also imparted the whole secret to successful technique, which whether working a church or bar or sidewalk consists of being relaxed, being oneself and expressing one's desires directly—and never, *never* communicating any hint of need. Gays can scent *need* a mile off, and they don't like it. *(Fear* is a different matter altogether.)

"It's all eye contact, Andy. The *eye* contact that goes on! But it's simple: See someone you like, turn your head away, then look back with *impact.*" Naturally I demonstrated. He jumped a mile.

"Not sure that's me, Ned."

Lighted a cigarette. "You're not attracted to men you run into? How about that kid at the library you told me about?"

"*Him!* Lost my books on purpose the other day!"

"I see. *Beware* the rage of the repressed homosexual. If he's put you in touch with your sexuality, he's done you great service. Be grateful, but be distant."

"Ned, I don't want to see someone and go to bed the very next thing. Doesn't that devalue the whole experience? I want to get to know him first."

I breathed smoke. "You're right," I said. "I know it. I gave up sex for that very reason."

"Gave up *sex?*"

"Worn out by it all, bored down to my toes by three decades of being trash. (There, I've told you my age.) It *is* a brutal kind of game, separating your dick from your heart."

"You're *celibate?*"

"Not any more – in theory, anyway. Turned my head around, and now when I have sex it's warm and meaningful, with somebody I like and respect. Not that it's as frequent as I'd like."

Stubbed out my cigarette and looked at him *hard.*

"Andy, do you find me attractive?"

Panic behind those glasses. Getting old is so humiliating. Had no doubt what his honest answer would be, but he seemed too nice, too polite to be candid.

And I was right.

"Sure," he said.

A worm crawled through my groin.

"Then I have a proposition to keep you out of trouble. See, I'm being upfront. You want to have sex right *now,* after putting it off your whole life, and outlets like parading nude across your airshaft don't do it for you." He blushed scarlet. "Don't want you to end up in jail, or for your first experience to be someone who'll chalk you up as just another trick. Billy drives me home. Why don't you wait and come with us?"

Seconds passed as I rubbed Dolly's ear. Now *my* heart was beating.

"OK," he said. "All right."

And I went to see who was rattling the door, which turned out to be Billy.

AFTER BILLY'S SESSION, we found Andy scanning a parish newsletter with the look of a man who's told a lie and now has to pay for it. Not unnatural that he wasn't fantasizing about sex with men my age; I understood *entirely*. But surely he saw that in my day I was handsome—even *very* handsome? The bones keep their place, even if the skin slips past. But though my white corduroys and slightly formulated hair deny it, my day was perhaps a while ago.

But I was confident that between Andy's legs were rebel stirrings at the idea of having sex right now, *tonight*. (Being young is so humiliating.)

Billy drove us west, his head turned to the backseat ("Library research! My God, how fascinating! I love to read! Do you like Tom Clancy?"). We fetched up across Ninth Avenue on 20th Street, the sky tracing pious outlines of steeples and gables.

After thanking Billy, I went indoors, turning on lights and floods and putting Dolly in the garden. Then I called to Andy to advance.

Mine's a beautiful apartment, a floor-through in a townhouse on Cushman Row, low rather than lofty, my few treasures displayed to advantage. I have taste—more taste than money, of course, but over time I've found one or two good things. That shining green garden makes an effective backdrop to my 18th-century English furniture, so masculine in its firm outlines.

Hung up his coat and installed him in the leather wingchair, handed him a glass of Jack Daniel's and sat down on the couch opposite. He looked around, impressed. I, too, savored my drink.

He pointed to a closed door. "Is that—the bedroom?"

"Living room. Never use it. I sleep in here. It's a Castro convertible."

"Why don't you use it?"

"It's—hard to explain. Took 20 years to furnish just the way I want. Some real prizes in there."

"Can't take it with you, you know."

"So they say, in the most malicious blow to human happiness ever delivered."

When Andy had drained his glass I pointed out several little Klees on the wall beside his chair, an angry Marsden Hartley. He stood up to see them better. Coaxing up my erection, I turned him around by the shoulders—he showed no resistance—and pressed my mouth and groin to his.

And what happened? His knees sagged. He'd kissed girls, but never a man, not even those he'd had sex with.

"Why don't you take off your clothes?" I murmured, and forthwith tossed cushions, pulled out the bed and undressed.

He piled his clothes on the chair and lay down. I slipped in nude next to him, and we kissed lying side by side. Then I ranged up over him. He liked the weight bearing down, even if my body was softer than his. We reversed positions and I pulled at his hips, gluing him to me and making him moan. Turned him on his back again, moving down until my mouth caught his cock. He arched, breathless.

When I came up for air, I said, "You have a very attractive cock, I *must* say."

"Wish it were bigger."

"It's fine. Bigger than mine."

Was this true? Investigating, Andy pressed his mouth to me and took me in.

"Uhh!" I said. "Let me show you what I like. Don't come in my mouth."

My slick mouth tasting him again, my hand squeezing while guiding my lips up and down, I put him on a spittle-thin film of sensation, the world sliding on the axis of his penis. How he groaned!

"Like *that,*" I said.

Andy did the same to me, getting more lost to himself, I expect, than ever in his life, forgetful of everything but my silk-textured stiffness, my slowly building moans. My contours caught his mouth in a perfect fit.

"When I come," I gasped, "don't move your head even half an inch."

And with a crisis of cries and springs and swells—and an iron clamp on his head—I frothed my splash in his mouth, for blissful seconds Lord of the Universe.

"Oh my," I managed at last. "Andy, you have a *talent.*"

"Thank you."

"No, no, thank *you.*" My hand found him again. "Do you use lubricant when you masturbate?"

"No."

"I'll show you." Squeezed lotion into my palm. "Jergens. I swear by it."

Coated him and began a slow, insistent, up-and-down squeeze, slowing at his moans, then speeding up, wrenching him to the bottom of his being, until in surrender white cords splashed his chest.

"*There.* Did you like that?"

He couldn't utter a word. After I sat up against the couch back and lighted up, he finally asked, "Aren't you supposed to feel sad after sex?"

"Maybe straights do, not us. So you enjoyed yourself?"

"*So* much."

"You'll be ready for springtime, when a young man's fancy turns to sex. I see you're ready for more, but I need my sleep. If you want, we can do it again next week."

"Not before?"

I considered. "I'll give you my number."

SOMEDAY WHETHER a boy's gay or straight will strike no one as being of more interest than whether he's blond or brunette, prefers baseball or football. There won't even be a name for an orientation so normal as gay. *Some* day. Will Manhattan Island still rise above the waters when that day comes? Not holding my breath.

Until the millennium, then, it's necessary for *somebody* to lay on the hands, introduce young gay men to the traditions they're heir to. Most work things out for themselves, but shame and guilt still trap so many others.

I revel in this surrogate fatherhood. It's my foremost satisfaction in being gay. Young men are touchingly grateful for attention, correction, approval and initiation; so unbelievably hungry for fathers. And why not? The profoundest truth I know is that a boy cannot grow up without one.

When I conceived of GRO, and secured from the Rev. Albright the use of a room in his parish house and recruited wise and experienced friends to help, I entered upon my true vocation: *fatherhood.*

A father's what I was meant to be all along. Coming out was natural for me—I don't mean this public confession that's *de rigueur* these days (if you have to confess it, can you feel so great about it?). When I seduced all but three of my fellow 7th graders (it's those three I still remember), I had no idea what I was doing was *coming out.* But after living as trash since age twelve, I find my salvation and redemption in counseling others—in giving back to the community. By now I have many sons.

Andy was not atypical of gay virgins, if a little older than most. His dad was one of those who never play catch with their boys, who pass up the joy of transmitting their manhood, take a hands-off approach to the most hands-on job there is. Go figure!

And his sexual nature was never acknowledged, much less encouraged (though you can't tell me even the densest parent doesn't *know*). Certainly he swallowed his father's attitude whole – grew up *despising* gay people, heard ringing in his ears for 26 years the great booming *No!* fathers install in their sons, so cruelly and gratuitously in their gay ones. It held him back, made him avoid people – kept him immature, and so naïve it seemed built-in.

But if he seldom dated, took several attempts to finish his education, shunned close friendships, why should Dad care? Life's hard, honey, get used to it. You're on your own. Sink or swim.

Someone has to clean up the mess. The worst cases we leave to the shrinks and jailers, but when people call GRO for help, we're there for them. Andy when he stumbled through our door was as estranged from himself and society as a not absolutely unhealthy person can be. In going to bed with me, he was affirming his identity as a gay man. My privilege was to be the agent of his release, to insure that his first experience came not at the untender mercies of the bars, but in my bed, under controlled conditions, me doing my feeble best to show him how loving gay sex can be.

Naturally it works both ways. That's the beauty of it. For me virgins are the most fun, and in this life you have to grab at what pleasures you can. Part of being human. And performing the oldest act there is? Keeps me young.

Plenty of men can't stand virgins, avoid them like the plague. I admit they never know what to do, and even when shown are not immediately proficient, but to me that's their charm. That nervous enthusiasm conquers me every time. No matter what he looks like, I'll go to bed with a virgin.

Sometimes from sheer overwhelmed *newness* they fall in love with me, or think they do. Those cases require a deft touch, for while conquest is fun, occupation's a bore. I disengage as nicely as I can.

Purists might disqualify Andy from virginity, what with his furtive few. But his entering my bed marked his debut in adult, consensual, guilt-free sex. That is the crucial difference; that's what I'm here for.

7. *No Floor of Roses*

LIFE WITH JAIME'S no floor of roses. It's cold there, and no water in the bathroom. Why? Because the landlord turned it off to the bathrooms so the drug dealer on the second floor would move out. But if Jaime and his girlfriend can flush the toilet with pans of water from the kitchen, can't he? Makes no sense. Anyway, he doesn't budge, so at least we never run out of weed.

The big problem is Miriam coming on to me.

One day Jaime's on his motorbike when a police car pulls up and squawks. Zooms into traffic; no warrant out that he knows of, but why take chances? So he zips down Fifth Avenue between cars and loses them, but they pick up on his vibe, radio ahead and cop cars come in from the side streets to block him.

Goes into evasive action, wrong way up one-way streets, through parking garages, across Union Square Park. No use. Skids on ice in front of a housewares store on West 14th, million cops running up with guns drawn as Jaime hits a rack of plastic bowls, rolls on the floor, throws up his hands and yells, "What I do? What I fucking *do?*"

Failure to signal turn, reads the first ticket, but there's plenty more, and they have to arrest him on account of evading arrest, not to mention his knife, so he's in a tank somewhere wedging his ass against the wall away from the rapists he's in with (except that evading arrest makes you popular) when Miriam makes her move.

What her problem is, I have no idea. Jaime's a little heavy, but he's a sexy guy. Accidentally ended up in bed with him myself once – not that anything *happened,* we were both laughing too hard – so I know he's got what it takes.

"Oh Eddie, I don' know what to do."

"Get a lawyer!" I tell her. "Bail him out!"

"He's changed," she goes. This is right after I get home, *hours* after Jaime's phone call, and all she's been doing is getting stoned and feeling sorry for herself. "Use to be so sweet. Like you, Eddie. My sweet little Jaime, I called him."

"Listen, you call his mother? Call his mother. Call Tia Luisa."

Goes on like that. But when a woman's made up her mind, there's nothing you can do. *Nothing*. Do what I can, and what does it get me?

"Must be *maricón,* Eddie. That's what everybody say, you know. I always say no way *Eddie's* faggot, no fucking *way,* but after this – "

Sorry, Jaime, man.

So when he gets sprung next day, I'm gone. Can't face my bro.

That's how I end up in Loisaida on Pablo's couch.

PABLO'S COUCH, *not* her bed, no matter how she begs. Wants to marry me, always has, and basically did save my ass in high school. Kids could call me *maricón,* but it was on spec: Bad at sports, late liking girls – late in general. Led to general suspicions. But Pablo was *flaming.* About Pablo there was never one second's doubt, not from the cradle, so she took the beatings *etc. etc.* that I and others I could name were spared.

She was 14 when she declared she was a woman trapped in a man's body.

I go, "Call *that* a man's body?"

So we're only engaged, and it's not going to come off until after the operation, and then only if it's a super success. Tell her, "I'm not putting my dick into no cut-rate shit."

"Feel this?" she says. "How silky? They turn it inside out, line my pussy with it. You'll *love* it."

"Better be some muscle in there."

"Squeeze you to a *straw.*"

Going to be a long engagement, because she keeps spending her operation money on clothes, and frankly I count on getting a place of my own before she gets her dick resectioned. But when she asks me to escort her on a glamorous night out, can't refuse. Owe her that much.

Rents me a tux, and a white Town Car picks us up. I say it's excessive.

"But I want to," she says, nervous in her tightest Angel Estrada.

Going down Greenwich Street the driver points out the girl working the corner. "See that?" he goes. "That's not a real woman. Must be a homosexual."

"No!" I go incredulously.

"Hee hee hee!" goes Veronica (her drag moniker). *"Hee hee hee!"*

For an extra two bucks, the driver gets out and comes around to open her door right in front of Desdemona's. Even checks his fly and tucks in his shirt, while Veronica discreetly makes the sign of the cross.

Knows how to make an entrance, give her that. Gets out

throwing not the teensiest look to anybody. Ten steps from curb to door, and in those ten steps Veronica: gives me her elbow with an appreciative glance, shepherds nonexistent stray hairs back into place, throws kissy faces to her friends and cuts her enemies dead ("Not Miss *Thing!*" under her breath), looks back in the car for her wrap, tugs a strap and checks the moorings of her right earring. Meanwhile the cha-cha queens squeal, "Who's your *husband,* Veronica? Who *is* he?" Which after all is the general idea, but I just sweep her in past the bouncer at the door.

Dark inside, and nasty-smelling. *Pounding* Supremes. Wouldn't you know, right off Veronica has to visit the little girl's room? I go up to the bar, order two vodka gimlets. It's what she drinks.

"I.D.?"

"I.D.?"

"How old are you?"

"Old enough.

"Need I.D."

So when Veronica makes grand entrance number two—charging in straight ahead, cheeks squeezed tight—I'm *steaming.* Fortunately they know her and give her the drinks.

Takes me to a table where friends are sitting. Searches her bag, takes out her gold cigarette case (plated), plucks out a cigarette, accepts a light from me (having previously passed me her gold lighter, also plated). Then she and a girlfriend repair to the little girl's room for more negotiations with the mirror. Take forever.

Sit in that velvet shrine and drink my drink, then hers also. Finally a friend of hers, Eugènè (née Floyd), pulls up close in a blue sequin number I politely compliment and buys me another. The streaks in her hair are a disaster, though, like a blond octopus is squatting on top of her head.

Veronica comes back and accuses me of flirting with Eugènè.

Persuade her otherwise with kisses and so on, and when Madonna comes on we even dance. Somehow I feel like I'm having a good time.

When she adjourns you-know-where for a touchup, Eugènè snakes up again. I've got another gimlet and I'm riffing away to the beat with big thoughts.

Which I decide to share. Ask Eugènè, "Know where bass gets you?"

"Where?" she answers ethereally.

"In your prostate, hits you right in your *prostate.*"

"I wouldn't know."

"What do you mean, you wouldn't know?"

"Girls don't have any."

"No prostate, my ass, *Floyd,*" I say.

"You s'posed to be *straight?*"

"Damn right I'm straight."

"Know what *I* think? *I* think you're *gay.*"

"The *fuck?*"

"You're about as straight as *Veronica.*" Who comes back just then. "Your 'husband,' he's *faggeaux,*" declares Eugènè. "He sucks *dick. Loves* it up the ass!"

Then the hair-pulling begins. Not much help in the fight. This is the night I find out how deceptive vodka is. Only a faggot would get mad, anyway. I do remember thinking, so *that's* why pocketbooks hang on chains.

When we get home, which I hardly remember, being drunk, I unfortunately forget to protest when Veronica folds me into her bed instead of the couch. She nestles in next to me, nude and slippery. Shaves all over.

"No sex," she warns, "or back you go to the couch."

"No worries."

"You can touch me," she says a minute later, bumping her ass against me, "if it helps."

What happens to my cock is only natural. Give her a pull for a joke, and she gets indignant.

"Stop it!" she says. "You're like all the rest! *Stop* it!"

"*You* stop it."

"Eddie, I said *no sex!*" In my ear: "Stop it!" Louder: "*Stop* it, Eddie!"

But I can't hear, because that's when I do what she never in eternity will forgive: I pass out.

8. *Plans "A" and "B"*

ANDY CALLED Saturday night, wanting to come over, but Saturdays are sacred to Wayne, my lover, so I told him I wasn't feeling well and would see him at church. As I feared he might, he sounded affectionate.

Went in Tuesday prepared, therefore, to begin to wrap things up. One more trip to bed might be about the limit. Didn't want him falling for me.

"The bars you're not ready for," I told him. "But there're some groups around town that should be just the ticket."

"You mentioned them."

"Sit around and rap about anything you like. *Much* better than standing at a bar throwing nasty looks around. The Lesbian and Gay Center has any *number* of groups. And did I mention the gay synagogue? *Everybody* goes."

But an unlooked-for pause. I crushed my half-melted peppermint.

"You know, Ned," he said, "it seems funny to go see a counselor and be taken to bed."

I'm used to it. Usually a late-night call from somebody barely coherent, "confronting" me (their word) after X number of months or years. Learned long ago, when someone tells you he wants to be honest with you, *run!*

"You *seduced* me!" they wail.

"Sorry you feel that way," I reply. "I can recommend a therapist if you want."

Not what they want, thank you very much. What they want is to rant on and feel sorry for themselves—have their cake and eat it, too. Might be the American way, but self-pity is my biggest bugaboo.

"You came to me for help when you found yourself up against something you couldn't handle by yourself," I remind them. "Did what I could."

Does that shut them up? Never.

"Takes two to tango," I point out.

Cuts no ice.

"I uncorked you—and *this* is the thanks I get?" And hang up.

Very unpleasant.

"Well, Andy, if you didn't *want* to, you should have said something."

"No, I wanted to—"

"From everything you told me, I said to myself, What this boy needs isn't *therapy,* it's *sex.* What with your airshaft exhibitions, I was afraid you'd land in *jail.*" Blew smoke expertly into the air. "Won't make any advances after this. I *had* hoped that after Billy's session—"

"Me too," he said, looking startled at his own words.

"Well, then?"

The phone rang. With concern I answered, "GRO. . . Hi, Billy, little late? We'll be here."

REMARKABLE HOW FEAR and shyness *vanish* the second time someone has sex. *Gone.* Novelty's good for one fun time in bed, guaranteed. After that, routine sets in. Andy was so cute the first time, so scared. But the second? Going for what he knew he liked. Gave him his blow job, lifting my head at the last minute and bringing him off by hand since I don't swallow. "It's the best I can do," I apologized. Then he sucked me off, again with talent.

Afterwards, smoking my cigarette, I delivered the sexual hygiene lecture my protégés always get.

Which left just one bit of unfinished business before Prof. Higgins kicked Eliza Doolittle out of bed. There was no need for Andy to look unattractive. If he cared to, he could look quite good indeed.

"You dress," I declared, "like a man your father's age."

"*You're* his age, and you don't dress like him."

"Exactly: You should dress more like me. Your appearance should reflect your new self-respect. Your cold-weather uniform should be corduroys—*snug*. For warm weather, chinos. And dark shirts with a light check."

Put on his glasses and wrote it down, saying my definiteness impressed him. "Why dark with a light check?"

"To modify that library pallor. Get a tan, Andy. Make that your project this spring. Your building have a roof?"

"Yes."

"Tar Beach, then." Hearing Dr. Kushner hiss in my ear, I added, "But don't get burned."

"Ned, my problem is I hate shopping. I judge shopping trips by how fast I'm out of the store. Last time, I was in and out of Bancroft with two pairs of pants and three shirts in ten minutes."

"So one sees," I said. "Most men don't like to shop, I don't know why."

"Men don't like thinking about their bodies—"

"Gay men are different, Andy. Gay men *like* their bodies and dress to show them off with something that says, I want to score."

"Writing that down: *I want to score.*"

"Andy, take off your glasses and let me look at you."

He removed the black frames.

"Lana Turner!" I said, more or less sincerely.

Glasses mar anyone's looks, but his case was extreme. He had a different—and handsome—face under there: Eyes bigger, bone structure more pronounced. As complete a change as I've seen.

"Lana Turner with a beard," I amended. "You'd look better, you know—more on the make—without the beard."

"I hate gay men's mustaches. Like signs spelling out *macho.*"

"Did I say anything about a mustache? Shave everything off, get a good haircut, you'd improve your looks *and* your chances."

But I missed whatever he said in response, for suddenly I had a *brainstorm!* One of those rapturous moments where all Creation goes clear!

"Speaking of chances," I said, "I have a young friend named Jay. Have I mentioned him?"

"No."

"Might like him. Might like *you*. Let me sleep on it. He's in med school, big exams coming up."

And of course Jay Stern had a pesky boyfriend named Denny. But Jay was an asset *waiting* to be activated to which I did not personally possess the key—but Andy *might*. Hence my excitement!

Jay had turned up at church two years before, on the verge of flunking out because repressing his sexuality was claiming all his energy. We got *that* squared away right off, not that he's much to look at. Of course, I'd never have *risked* alienating him had he let drop sooner that his father's the one publisher of literary fiction I really admire (never mind the money he rakes in from movie-star tell-alls). Believe me, after that tidbit came to light, Jay got the kid gloves.

He and Andy were both bright, decent men. Once Andy's appearance got spruced up (Jay wouldn't be caught dead with anyone half so homely as himself) they might go for each other. I did have Denny's grapple hooks to contend with; those swishy blonds make worthy antagonists.

But *if* the Denny problem could be solved, and *if* Jay and Andy turned out to be a match made in heaven, enormous benefit could accrue all around, for a publishing career might be the answer for Andy: A way of congenially keeping his distance from the world while being usefully connected to it. Grubbing around libraries? He could do better.

So call it Plan *"A"*—rather, Plans *"A" and "B."* Plan *"A"* for *Andy*: Give Andy the right career. Plan *"B"* for *Boyfriends*: Give Andy a boyfriend and Jay the *right* boyfriend (that Denny was the very *wrongest).* Upshot of either plan worked correctly: My novel would nab itself (eventually, but Patience is my middle name) a publisher. Win, win, win!

If I'm a saint, there's nothing wrong with a saint's being resourceful. In this wicked world?

For my book was done—virtually *done*—but had no publisher in prospect. *Mixed Signals* represents everything of me. Into it I have poured, pounded and stamped every morsel of what I don't lightly (if also not without irony) call wisdom, transmuted into fiction by—*dammit!*—by *art*.

I harbor no illusions it'll be a best seller, or even favorably reviewed by the light minds that do such chores nowadays (reserving their rapture for murder mysteries, God save us! I'd write one myself, but my nature lacks the requisite cruelty). No, my allergy to uplift sentences it, at best, to the dusty shelf dourly labeled *Literature.*

What I count on is the process always at work, inexorable as the glaciers, grinding away to bring to the surface those few works that *cannot* be crushed to chaff—the *classics*—as surely as my skin pushes up its crop of moles.

Mixed Signals is my masterpiece, and in order to get it published, all's fair. All's fair in love and war and *art.* I cannot, *will* not die until it's out. Once it is, who knows if I'll even linger for the book tour? When dying's such a shot in the arm for sales?

Those were the stakes, then: The *highest.* Just thinking about it gave me the heebie-jeebies.

"Ned, would you take me shopping? *Please?*"

Made me jump. I'd forgotten about Eliza Doolittle. But I am such a pushover.

"Saturday do? Meet you across from Jefferson Market Library at noon. Wait, you're checking out rap groups Saturday—"

"Not this weekend," he said. "Not yet."

"Saturday, then. We've had a nice time, but you should be getting home. How you do research keeping *these* hours—"

"Can't I spend the night?"

"*No,*" I said. "I can't sleep with anyone in my bed. Now remember, Andy, up to you whether we do this again or not."

He hesitated visibly. Oh, they're all alike. After I had a better time than expected, too.

9. *Hell Day*

WEDNESDAY'S MY HELL day. Shift runs 10:00 to 6:00, then dash up to City College hanging my chin on somebody's shoulder and wheezing on the steel filings. My asthma doctor says stay out of the subway, but what can I do? Two classes back-to-back in the new building that looks like a prison. Through sealed windows it gives us convicts a view of the old campus, covered with ivy like it's Yale. An hour of French (which reminds me more and more of Chemistry), then my English Honors seminar. *Oy!*

But I love that seminar. Only seven of us, and Prof. Godalming himself teaches it, but what a way to end the day, and wouldn't you know, my turn to make a presentation. Godalming runs it like grad school, everybody takes turns. All day every minute I can I'm brushing up on Hawthorne.

After French crawl exhausted up to the seminar room. Beth's already there. She's a super-A student, a writer who's had stories rejected by *The New Yorker*. Meet at an English Club party. Everybody else brings potato salad, I take a plate of stuffed finger things from a Russian deli. Beth picks one up, takes a bite, makes a face, puts it back.

Cool! I go up and make friends right away.

"Are you Jewish?" she asks.

"From the waist down," I assure her. (Someone told Mami it was the law in America. Mutilated at eight years old!)

That's how our thing started. The first time I swear she raped me. Women do more raping around than they take credit for. But she's pretty, and also the first girl I ever met with a trust fund.

"Hey, Eddie," she goes. "You ready?"

"As I'll ever be. Deceptive story."

This amuses her. She's old for an undergrad. Sit two chairs away, but she puts her feet in my lap until I go, *"Don't."*

Everyone trails in. English courses are my favorite, but they do get the weirdos. Start to get nervous until Godalming arrives. He's great. White, has his white family, brings the Mrs. to every occasion, but lives with his Black girlfriend and their kids. He's always encouraging me.

The usual announcements, then he looks over, checking I'm good to go. Give him the nod, and he says, "Well, continuing in our New England mode, this week it's Eduardo's turn. What is it, again?"

Says that so I can grab some air.

"*My Kinsman, Major Molineux,* by Nathaniel Hawthorne," I reply, and everybody turns their guns on me. English majors will jump you at the first sight of blood.

"Well, this story's very deceptive," I start, pleased to get a nod out of Godalming already. "Basically it's an initiation myth, OK? This kid Robin comes to town looking for his rich cousin Major Molineux, but finding him becomes this ordeal to prove his manhood, OK?

"The minute the ferryman puts him off—I spare you any reference to Charon—" I add cleverly, "he has his first symbolic encounter: Meets this old man who refuses to say where the cousin is. Same thing in a tavern, plus the innkeeper puts him down, says he must be a runaway servant," I say significantly. Everybody in there but Beth, Godalming and me is Black. "Message: Without his cousin, Robin's *nobody*. He leaves pissed, ready to mug someone—'with lifted cudgel,' OK?—and meets this whore. She wants to initiate him herself, but he's too innocent to know what's going on, he just leaves.

"It's obvious everybody knows his cousin, but no one cops to it. It's like"—and here I get carried away—"like if I go to Cuba, ask around for my father, everyone would say, 'Sure, like *you* could be the son of Havana's leading doctor, Fidel's best friend! As *if!*'

"So then Robin hallucinates his family sitting around wondering how his quest's going. That's like he's saying goodbye to boyhood, because now he meets a guy who says, 'Major Molineux? He's coming!' This mob with torches and musicians comes up, and lording it over everybody from his place of honor on a cart is Major Molineux himself."

What's Beth's problem, sitting there grinning?

"Robin's eyes lock on his kinsman's in like a transfer of *manhood*: The end of the quest. Robin's a warrior now, too, replacing his cousin, whom they carry off in—I love Hawthorne's phrase—in 'tar-and-feathery dignity.' 'Tar-and-feathery,' like the Major's spirit knows it's time to fly away, but *tarries,* too, OK? And Robin—note his own feathery name—Robin's learned that though it's nice having rich relatives, in this life you have to find your *own* road, OK?"

Tidy my notes while everybody looks at Godalming to see what to think. *I'm* happy.

"Fascinating, Eduardo," he says. "Finding magical realism in *Hawthorne!* Seems a promising approach."

Uh-oh. Hell, I collapse. I know what *promising* means.

"Some background information might enrich our interpretation," he goes on. "A key to the story—in *my* reading—lies in the first paragraph, the narrator lamenting how the king's usurped—taken over—powers earlier granted the colonies? There's a fissure—a gap—between the people and the sovereign power, OK? So as Robin searches for his kinsman, we already suspect Cuz's hold on power might be shaky, OK?"

OK, OK already. Everyone nods dumbly, like they give a fuck.

"Now let's examine that phrase. 'Tar-and-feathery dignity' is what we call a self-destructing artifact, OK? 'Dignity' refers to royal power, but 'tar-and-feathery' undoes it, *mocks* it, because how they used to disgrace somebody was to tie him to a fence rail or cart, strip him, pour hot *tar* over his body and dump *feathers* on the tar, not omitting to jam a spray up his, uh" – and he nods at *me!* – "anus. So tarring and feathering Robin's uncle is a kind of lynching – "

Thank God! *That* sets them off. *Furious* outcry about how tarring-and-feathering can't compare to *lynching*. Godalming goes he *agrees*, he *agrees*, we're talking about the same *thing*, while gradually I decide not to kill myself.

Finally the bell goes. Everyone jumps up, Godalming looks glad as hell and Beth grabs my shirt.

"Eddie, that was brilliant! Let's go talk – "

Who needs that patronizing crap? This from a girl who wants to devote her life to the peasants of Central America!

"Just remembered, I'm late."

Run out of there and jump on the train for Pablo's.

10. *Sheer Inspiration*

WHAT HELD ME up that Saturday, left Cinderella stranded on the sidewalk, was no small thing. A writer lives for the energy that gets words on paper. Torrents of it may seize some few every day – your Maugham, your Saroyan, your Mailer (at what cost, I needn't say) – but for others of us it's a more fugitive infusion.

Mixed Signals had been 17, 18 years in the writing and wasn't done yet. Oh, nominally it was finished, lying on my sunroom table first page to last, but in my heart I knew the ending was wrong, *ruined* the book. Not that I could put my finger on the problem.

I know how futile *17 years* sounds. The only thing that kept me going is the conviction that my stuff's *good*—hard-won but golden. What price Maugham, when no one reads him? An *ounce* of pure gold outweighs a *ton* of plate any day (something like that; never pays to get fancy).

But it's been agony. Writing's already the hardest work you can do; every word weighs a ton. And a book's the author's open wound until it's published, when it can finally close up and heal; until then the very air stings. And if in the meantime the morsel of life force one seeks to encapsulate gives up the ghost. . . A 17-year crisis.

So it was a gift from heaven to wake up that Saturday *knowing* what to do. Sheer inspiration, which normally I don't believe in. Tore up the last 20 pages (metaphorically; in actual fact, laid them in my safe for the benefit of future scholars). Tore up 20 pages, and wrote four new ones.

That it was the right ending, I knew *instantly,* and added the two words I'd despaired of ever sincerely writing:

THE END

The letters rose monolithic, a littler Stonehenge. Printed out my pages and placed them at the end of the manuscript. Then sat there, depleted. *Nothing* left in me, hardly the energy to squash the cockroach that came waltzing out of an early chapter.

Naturally I forgot about Andy. An artist has to use his energy while it flows. That's the rule.

Standing up a free man, I went into the bathroom and peered

into my only mirror (it's years since I put my looking-glass on the curb to punish its want of tact; within five minutes a young beauty bore it away, looking pleased. I wish them well). What had 17 years of servitude done to me?

When I started *Mixed Signals* I was hardly off my juicy prime. In youth, the skin swells to contain (barely!) the eager life growing within it, which expresses itself in shapes precise, personal, decorative. Then it begins to shrink. Wrinkles mark the retreat. The grave has an invisible imperative only artists can fight free of, and then only for a time.

Invisible? I wish. No accident *grave* and *gravity* have the same root. But why must the tomb receive us half-rotted? Why such pointless economy? I won't speak of its painful electrolysis on the pate, nor of the obscene puckering around the nether regions (but why, Lord? *Why?*). The *most* discouraging thing is to reach down and lift up a flatworm that used to be springy and resistant.

Sex tortures you for years and years, then you wish it would.

Slowly I shmushed my face into the glass, seeking just a *glimpse* of youth. Time had melted me, puddled me, dried me out—but *completely?* If ever I lose *every* attribute of youth, I won't *know* myself. I used to be young, how can *I* ever get old? The last, infallible sign? When I can't get it up; by their nature erections are young. Doesn't my potency *show?*

Forcing my pupils into one black Cyclops eye, I dove through the window of my soul—fell in, yet kept dry, a more successful Narcissus: *For youth remained.* I could feel the years slipping off me like skin off a snake. A matter *always* of bone structure.

The telephone rang.

"Ned, I've been waiting half an hour!" Andy wailed. "Did you forget?"

To put aside the bliss of achievement to show a kid how to

dress! It was a growling old bear he finally saw shambling down Sixth Avenue that freezing afternoon.

I apologized profusely, explained that inspiration had struck with my novel, and eyed him top to toe. Hair, disaster. Beard and glasses, ditto. And his clothes! What was he *thinking*? Stood there in a parka without shape, a shirt like a barber's smock, pants like galvanized drainpipe. Whereas we were in Greenwich Village, Manhattan, confident, sexy people going past with all the right moves.

Sighed, and went to work.

And two stores later, I had the satisfaction of seeing a butterfly emergent, half-gummed still but already pleasing to look at in corduroys and subtly checked shirt. In gratitude, he pressed me to let him buy me lunch. And I relented! Lent patience by the thought that dispensing some final pointers would finish off Eliza Doolittle before I had a stroke.

After fending off questions about my novel, I asked between mouthfuls, "Did you see that salesman? The way he rolls up his sleeves? You should do that. Makes the muscles look firmer."

"I like short sleeves."

"No, short sleeves look funny. Long sleeves, but when it's warm, roll them up or the sight of you will make people uncomfortable. You have to look cool in summer and warm in winter or people won't like it." He didn't get it. "Andy, we dress for other people. That's the whole trick of it."

"But—"

"The *world* sets the terms, *you* don't, and neither do *I*. This self-consciousness of yours: Don't you see how self-conscious is *not* the same as self-aware? *Crucial* to realize that."

So crucial I must have raised my voice, for the ladies in the next booth turned their heads, forks suspended.

"So help me, Andy, I don't see the *threat* in shopping for a new outfit. *What?* I can't hear you."

"These clothes make me feel nude."

"Get over it. You're ashamed of your body because it's *sexual*, let alone *homosexual*, but you have a perfectly *sexy*—" Broke off to glare next door. They got busy with their salads.

As though a greasy burger's ever a good idea. My colon started to spasm. My cousin's colitis made her life not worth living.

At the door I saw a boy with a reasonably sensitive face who momentarily knocked Plan *"B"* out of my head.

"*That's* the kind of guy you should meet," I said loudly—for all the good it did.

On the sidewalk Andy's lips moved, but I couldn't hear a thing. "Are you saying something?"

In a whisper: "Are my pockets lumpy?"

Christ! Stopped to look.

"Don't stop!"

"No, they're fine," I said evenly. "In New York you have to wear your wallet in front. Breaks the line, but you have to."

"OK."

"Andy, this is the limit," I went on. "I'm glad our expedition was a success, you look good, but I'm too old and ill to be giggled at by an over-aged adolescent in the heart of the Village. Hope I've helped you, but you're ready to leave the nest and face the world. Or you better be, because I don't want to see you again."

He stood, a tableau of shock, one shopping-bag-laden arm held out at an unlikely angle like a broken wing.

"You're dropping me?"

"I'm not *dropping* you," I said with real annoyance, since that's exactly what I was doing.

"See, this is what puts me off about gays," he said, lucid for the first time all day. "They insist on being in a snit."

"I am *not* in a snit," I began, but I was telling it to snugly-clad buttocks pumping expressively away.

11. *Big Fat 2%*

Heading off to work when this *angel* carrying up the *Times* and *Daily News* passes me on the stairs. *Hey,* it's that Andy-Tommy dude!

"Hi!" I go. "Nice duds! You *live* here?"

"Morning," he grunts, then looks at me. *"Hi!* You work at the Library!"

No shit, Sherlock. Swear his voice goes up an octave. At the Library we aren't even nodding to each other anymore. But I hear myself offer to wait a mo, go uptown with him.

Linger in his front room while he's in the bathroom. Bare—desk, TV, couch. Library call slips spill around the Mac. When he comes out I'm studying his Oxford English Dictionary, micrographic edition.

"Love this!" I say. "Hey, there's a bullet hole in your window! *Cool!*"

"I didn't know you lived here."

"Staying upstairs? Temporarily? With my friend Pablo Escondido?"

"Don't think I know him."

"Veronica?"

"The drag—?"

"The pre-op, that's her."

"She seems sweet." Loads up his pockets with call slips and pencils. "I've held the door for her."

"Very sweet, but she packs a knife, you know."

We grin at each other. "Well, I'm set. What's your name, anyway?"

"Edward."

"Andrew." Like I didn't know it already.

As we step outside, a Latino shouldering a boombox passes and we follow to the classic beat of *I Will Survive.* Spring-like February day, lacy light falling off the fire escapes. Don't say much as we go along – don't have to, which is nice. At Avenue B a little boy walking backwards bumps into me. "Sorry," he says softly, going his backwards way. The Tompkins Square Park playing field is empty blue asphalt, its fence silver netting. When the music cuts off, we stumble and laugh.

A garbage truck, Teddy bear hanging from a noose on the grille, is angled at the Boys Club door on Avenue A. In its shadow a street person lowers his pants and squats.

"That's *disgusting!*" I go loudly.

Ask about his job and he tells how following hints from Terse's diary through books and microfilm makes every day like Christmas.

"Cool!" I go.

"I always start with the British Library catalog. A lot of the people Terse mentions published books, so I can find their full names and go on from there."

Near First Avenue kids who should be in school are sitting on a stoop.

"Hey, Clark Kent!" one calls.

"Hey, this guy passes every day!"

"Hey, *Superman!*"

We ignore them. Pass a punk mama holding hands with a pink-haired tyke of four and its green-haired twin. A businessman comes at us talking into a chunky cell phone with that dumb *"I'm*-on-the-phone-and-you're-*not"* look. At Second Avenue I point out a sign – *Madame Espinosa E.S.P.* – and go, "Like it's a graduate degree."

Turn the corner at Grace Church, its marble melting with age. On the slate sidewalk two sexy guys stand in the sun, the shirtless one trapping a German Shepherd between his legs. When it whimpers at a pigeon, he launches it with a thrust of his hips.

"Don't get the wrong idea," I tell Andrew. "Pablo's just giving me a place to crash. I'm not gay."

"That's cool, *I* am," Andy-Tommy tells the world.

"Am what?"

"Gay. *Queer.*"

My mouth must fall open, I see it in his faggot face. "Hey, just remembered! *See*-ya!" And I run through a group of deaf kids signing to one another and laughing uproariously, up to 14th Street and down the subway steps.

What are they, 2% of the population? Big fat 2% when every guy I meet turns out to be one! And to tell me straight out! Has he no shame? Can just see him in pink hot pants at their Gay Pride Parade, blowing kisses up Fifth Avenue.

But fuck! Why does every guy I like have to be a faggot?

FEW DAYS LATER, Pablo reminds me nothing's for free in this life. Makes no bones what she's after, and won't take no for an answer.

"I don't go that way."

"Same thing, Eddie."

"Same thing, my ass."

"*My* ass. Put it in, take it out, how's that any diff—?"

"You're *gross.*"

"What else you do around here? Sweep? Do laundry? Wash the dishes?"

"Where's the vacuum, I'll—"

"Sweep *me*, baby."

I really can't fucking stand it when the gestures get going. Had to put up with this shit since the funny thing that happens in high school, one day you're a stick jumping all over the place trying to be seen, the next you walk down the hallway and girls' heads go *snap! snap! snap!*

Fling my key at the bitch and stamp up to the roof. Have to figure out where to go. Several girls would welcome me, but with strings. Nothing's decided when the roof door opens an inch, then wider, and Veronica, flowered quilt over bra and panties, teeters over the tar on those damn red heels. Sits on the parapet, giving me her best profile while she gazes at the Empire State Building. I stick with my view of Brooklyn or whatever.

"Look at the Empire State, Eddie! Someone sewed on a thousand silver sequins!"

"Those are called windows," I inform her.

"Fuck, making me break my lease," she says. "Says no high heels on the roof."

I glare, but have to know. *"Why?"*

"Leaks. There." She kicks them off and reaches her claws over. "It's my fault, hon, I get so crazy—"

I can stay, and don't have to fuck her either: She'll settle, she tells me, for having her heart broken by the sexiest man in New York.

FINE. BUT A WEEK later she freaks out, same day this *guy* follows me home from work, some creep making every turn 20 steps behind me. When I reach my stoop, end of the line, I turn to give a nod of dismissal, of *game's over, go away.*

Imagine how I feel turning around to find hot on me the eyes of Andy-Tommy, the known queer from downstairs, no beard or glasses and gayer than ever!

"Didn't recognize you," I go.

Asks do I want a drink!

Turn that down, asks for my number! At least I have the

presence of mind to give him Mami's, not Veronica's.

Naturally when I get upstairs Veronica's strung out and trashing the place. Last thing you need, end of the day, tired, reading to catch up on, not even your own place, but have to act interested in someone wearing panties that separate her balls and tuck her penis between them so she's flat as a woman, is to come home and find her smashing everything she owns with Spanish maledictions. Place is knee deep in broken *tchotchkes.*

I've had enough. Stuff my pack and call home from the corner. Luckily Mami answers.

"¿Mi querido hijo, cómo estás?"

Good timing. Thank God for drug sweeps! They had one in our building, she says, troop of guys in DEA letter jackets running through. They busted Suriya's mom, and Suriya moved out, and also even before that Mami saw her hanging out lovey-dovey with her old flame Tito (also busted), which sounds a hell of a lot more like her than the accidental thing we had going.

So I can go home, but there's a catch: José suddenly comes up with a son my age named Joselito, fresh from Argentina, and Joselito has my room. Mami says he's very nice, which tells me what to expect.

Go uptown immediately. Mami hugs me and cries, unusual for her, which oils my way back in. José's idea is the living-room couch, but there's a cot from when his brother stayed with us before sentencing that we put in my room—for *me,* not the scrawny interloper. Who says not two words from behind José.

But home's home. Finally I have different clothes and only blocks to walk up the hill to City College—my shining City upon a hill.

12. *How to Score Tonight*

When weeks passed—the pear trees on my block were budding!—and Andy hadn't called, I felt so *reckless*—my God, my ticket into *print!*—that I called up his boss, Professor Onorato of Columbia University, to say I wished to get in touch with his research assistant Andrew (whose last name I fudged, since I didn't know it) regarding the position, and left my number. A hint of headhunter machinations never hurts.

This was the very tippy-top time of *We're No. 1!* The Gulf War a glorious success, for a few days Saddam Hussein looked terrified, as though if we bothered to send a Humvee to Baghdad, he'd surrender. But we don't bother. My feelings were mixed. I was drafted and served stateside during the Korean War; best sex I ever had, but otherwise a bore.

That evening my phone rang.

"Hello, Ned," said a voice from the far side of the moon.

I apologized, and Andy more than met me half way with such eagerness I ended up inviting him over.

Arrived out of breath. I reared back to take a good look at him: a new, *sexy* man! Clean-shaven, good haircut, contact lenses—nothing left of the frump I met. *You do good work,* I told myself.

"Let go, Handsome, have to let Dolly in. Oh yes, you do look good."

"Oh Ned."

Sat him down and, as he berated his childishness on our shopping trip, reached to his knee.

"Forget about it, Andy. Water under the bridge. Your redeeming quality is that you have a loving heart."

Hope I didn't grimace saying that. Might have.

"Learn from this, that's all I ask. Know what's what before you invest emotion.

"Andy, you never ask me questions. I have a lover. Never in my wildest dreams did I think *I* would fall in love, but I met Wayne six years ago. *Nothing* when I met him, and now he's a personal trainer. He's the only man I've ever said 'I love you' to."

"Then why – ?"

"We have an arrangement. Wayne comes over Saturday night. For the rest, I never ask – though he always tells. If *I* didn't sleep around, he'd wonder why he's with an old man nobody wants."

"How old is *he?"*

"What's *that* got to do with the price of tea in China? No spring chicken. Pushing 30."

Andy's body slumping, eyes heavy, I thought *poor baby.* Not everybody his age could feel things so much. How can I be a cold person when sweetness turns me on? Certainly hadn't planned it.

"Would you like to go to bed, Andy?"

"Oh yes."

Kissed him, and things went on from there.

AFTERWARDS, TOUCHING a match to my cigarette, I gave Plan *"A"* a nudge.

"You know, I worry about you, shuffling through the bowels of libraries while Professor Pastrami reaps the glory."

"I like it."

"High time you thought about life after Terse. Why didn't they do him a generation ago, anyway? Isn't it late in the day for the second-rate Victorians?"

"Ned!"

"My point is, the *you* who buries himself in that stuff is the *old* you. You're *out* now, living in the light of day. You tunneled away from the world when you thought you were worse than other people—if also better—but *neither's* true: You're just like other people. Whatever the sins of society, you *have* to join in. Being on the sidelines hasn't made you happy, so I don't see why you resist. Figure out what you *do* want and go for it. Ultimately, what matters more to a man than his career?"

"What do you think I should do?"

"Why not think about *publishing?* Not much money at first, but once you find a good book and see it through—"

"Guessing best-sellers, Ned? Sounds dreary."

Plan *"A"* took a hit, but no point arguing.

"Well, with your research skills you could go right to *ORBS* Magazine or FORTUNE, some place like that, make a real living doing what you enjoy."

"Maybe," he said with interest. "Maybe, when the time comes. . ."

Plan *"A"* recovered. Carom shot. But a saint with only one arrow in his quiver can end up a pincushion like St. Sebastian.

The thing about these media giants is their publishing divisions. For instance, OrbsCorp has two book arms, Foster & Hatch and OrbsBooks. My preference would be Foster & Hatch—an old firm, numinous still—but OrbsBooks would do!

No doubt Andy was a brilliant researcher, but I didn't see him happy endlessly fact-checking magazine articles. No, as an introvert whose more vivid life is that of the imagination, he'd *blossom* shepherding writers into print. Had publisher written all over him.

Well, then: Get him to *ORBS*. Six months there, a year—however long it takes to find he doesn't like it—and a lateral move to Foster & Hatch. There he'd find himself an editorial assistant who needs to discover a salable book in order to advance. Some do this by discovering the new Judith Krantz (the new Judith Krantz we have always with us), but the best look for something more. And when they find it, they go to the wall for it.

There was the possibility Andy wouldn't like *Mixed Signals*. Someone of his inexperience? But a boy, I felt sure, of sturdy loyalties.

The alternative? Sending the manuscript over the fanged transoms of agents and publishers into the quicksands of their slush piles. Please God, save me from that!

"What does Pastrami pay you?"

"I wish you wouldn't—"

"Sorry. Well?"

"Twelve dollars an hour."

"You *live* on that? At a top magazine you'd double that right off, in time do very well. I'm not introducing you to the *glossiest* gay lifestyle, but you'll want to keep up your wardrobe and so forth, which takes—"

"Tell me about your novel, Ned."

Oof! Was I that obvious?

"Don't know what to say, Andy, except that it's the distillation of my life's experience."

"I'd love to read it."

"Thanks, let me think about that."

"What have you published?"

Fussed with another cigarette.

"Andy, my tragedy is I'm a writer of fiction who's never published any. I mean, I've reached print: Wrote a handbook years ago."

"That's terrific!"

He sounded relieved, dammit. People can never stand it when they learn you're a writer. Challenges come high ("What have you written that I might be familiar with?") and low (my favorite being my old cleaning lady's, "Don't you get tired of *sitting?"* (the answer is yes)). Apparently turning out a literary masterwork is something anyone could do if only they thought it worth their while. Meanwhile, *your* giving it a shot affronts them.

"What kind of handbook?"

"A slender volume called *How to Score Tonight*. Did well, thank God, or I'd be on welfare."

"How to Score Tonight?"

"The how-to section? Worth *gold."*

"How'd you come up with it?"

"One day, back in the Dark Ages, the Seventies – *Dark* Ages, did I say? The *Golden* Age for gay people – I got to thinking, *What* has sex with 2,000 men taught me? *What* – "

"How many?"

"By now it must be closer to – "

"Jesus! Two thousand men!"

"You make it sound like millions. Trust me, it was going from one boredom to the next."

But he went on and on. Well, I'd put him on the royal road, right? If he wanted.

"If you're finished. . ." I said. "I put down what I know about what men like, types that attract types, how to cruise – *everything*. Spilled my thimbleful of knowledge, hoping to help cut through the bullshit, cause less rejection, contribute to a better gay self-image. Nothing wrong with that, is there?"

"No, no."

"Told you, used to be trash. This was before AIDS, you understand, when the only price one paid for promiscuity was psychic – the one currency I can keep track of. Thinking of updating it, actually. Maybe you could help with the research?"

"I'd like to read it," he said cautiously.

"Believe me, Andy, you're getting the benefit without having to shell out 9.95 or whatever."

When I closed the door on him—after an unprecedented three trips to bed with a coming-outer—at least Old Man Conscience was eased.

A FEW WEEKS LATER Jay Stern called up to complain that Denny was refusing him sex until he settled certain spiritual matters Jay couldn't make head nor tail of. The last time they *had* made it to bed, Denny proudly displayed his unmoved parts hanging off him—Jay said angrily—like soft pink shit. Upshot: They were taking a time-out.

I was delighted! Trying to separate two people is usually the best glue going, but now I didn't even have to try. Which at last gave me an opening to promote Plan *"B"* for *Boyfriends,* because I judged that Andy's recent one-night stands were working some of the mushiness out of his system.

Yes, Andy-boy was venturing out to gay bars on their packed two-for-one-nights, and there daring to approach sexy young men—though to do so, he told me, caused a hush to fall and a spotlight to follow him through a parting crowd to any object of his lust so unwary as to have returned his gaze, no one breathing until they saw how he fared. (As he said, he might have conquered fear, but now was meeting anxiety: *"Do I look OK?")*

He had some luck, too, but soon was denouncing the bar scene like everybody else. Waking up beside random attractive youths, he complained, wasn't helping him in what he proclaimed his life's aim of finding a lover.

He did allow that casual sex was fun.

"Stop the presses!" I said.

Thus my advice to Jay.

"There's only one road to *Denny's* heart, and that's the highway bypass," I told him. "Go straight at him and he'll happily torture you till kingdom come. Look at someone else and he'll *hound* you."

Jay seeming to take it in, I told him my young friend Andy was eager to meet him.

Then called Andy to say Jay wanted to meet *him*.

At first he balked.

"You said Jay *has* a boyfriend, Ned."

"That's over, and Denny's left him a *wreck*. *You* could save him."

"How?"

My answer was a principled one he had to respect.

"By being his friend, his *true* friend. That Denny only promoted episodes of high drama. Got bored otherwise, and why not? *He's* boring. Nothing tires me more than a gorgeous flower in love with himself, but really so self-hating he makes *your* life an ordeal of every day having to prove your love anew. Don't tell Jay, but Denny was a real problem between us. I neither approved nor understood."

"If you didn't understand, what faith can I put in your strategy for saving him?"

"Andy, that's the first really astute question you've asked me! I swear, it confirms my faith in *you*.

"I've no guarantees to offer," I went on, "but I know Denny was no friend to that boy. Gave him all the pain he could contrive, required that Jay reach across the flames of hell to him. Wouldn't believe in his affection otherwise."

"And doesn't Jay perhaps require to be tortured?"

"Astute question number two! And the answer is, maybe so. He's on a mission to give of himself, all right. I only hope he figures out it's as a *doctor* he should do it, not sacrifice his whole life.

"You may lack Denny's cheap flash, Andy, but you're more than presentable, and Jay goes for *shiksas*. My intuition tells me you're a match – I'm talking genuine connection. Far be it from me to *interfere,*" I said (yes, he laughed), "but I couldn't wish a better fate for Jay than you, or a better one for you than Jay."

Andy said he'd call him. "No big deal. Dinner if he wants, stroll around. Maybe back to my place or his, if – you know."

"Might lay in dessert if you want to get him to yours."

"Where's he live, anyway?"

"Washington Heights."

A silence, as seemed appropriate. I've never been; who has?

ANDY DID CALL Jay, they did have dinner and went dancing, too – a big step for Andy-boy, since if he'd dressed to deny his body until the day before yesterday, why would he ever have wanted to move that body rhythmically in public?

They went to the current hot disco, in a neighborhood I associate with printing presses, down into a brick-walled space where go-go dancers posed atop columns, spotlights cutting off their heads like so many Apollo Belvederes and the dance floor resounding with ear-splitting whistles.

When they adjourned to Tiffany's on Seventh Avenue for breakfast, Jay told Andy he was nervous about having to start doing physical exams for school. Andy volunteering to let him play doctor, they headed uptown, where Jay pressed his stethoscope to him, peered into his more polite orifices and they had sex.

"I'M A MATCHMAKER!" I said, getting Andy's report. Not that it's a strain guessing a good-looking kid will pick up a taste for seduction. "Better than being with an old man, isn't it?"

A pause he suddenly tried to work his way out of. I *laughed.*

"What did you talk about?"

"This and that. Life in the closet. Oh, and you."
"Me?"
"Jay told me everything.
Had to wonder what version of *everything* that might be.

13. *My Dear Father*

ONE NIGHT José and Joselito are out who knows where when Mami's sister Isabel calls. A telephone call from Cuba! Letters in a blue moon—*never* the phone.

Isabel does all right for herself, she's a teacher, studied in Russia. Wants to say hello to me, but I refuse on principle. For Mami it's a call from another lifetime. Brought me up on stories about Havana's glamorous cars and nightclubs, meeting Ernest Hemingway. Never talks about my father. What kind of unmarried woman gives herself to a man? OK, here it's *chic* to have kids and no husband, here you're a *star*, but in Cuba you're a *whore*.

That's how we end up in New York. Get on a boat, land in Florida three days later. Settle in Miami, where Cubans get rich? Not us, too easy. Mami has a sin to expiate: *Me*. So we wind up on the edge of Harlem, and Mami finds the perfect job at the seminary. Gives her plenty of time on her knees, scrubbing floors. Just to keep her sins fresh, José moves in. I can hear their disgusting animal noises through the wall.

On the phone she and Isabel go on forever, Mami weeping

away, when she writes something down and hands me this soggy scrap that's our first-ever address for my father. What his relationship is with Isabel I can imagine.

So I sit down at the kitchen table and write:

April 4, 1991

My dear Father,

I presume to call you such because I am your son by Sereña Polanco y Martinez. I am 19 years old and an Honors student in my sophomore year at the College of the City of New York, majoring in English Literature and minoring in Classics. I also work at the New York Public Library. I intend to become a professor or a writer.

My mother is well. She is in her 11th year of work at Union Theological Seminary.

My aunt Isabel has given us your address, and it gives me joy to know that this letter will reach your hands. Although there has never been communication between us, I hope I carry myself in such a way that you can take pride in

your son,
Eduardo de Quesada

Flowery, but that's Spanish.

Show it to Mami. Ecstatically she reads it to Isabel, and weeps another river. It's dripping tears when she hands it back. Fan it dry, stuff it in an envelope, plaster on the stamps, run downstairs and mail it. Hang out, and when I'm back Mami's off the phone at last, bent over the table crying her eyes out.

If that call's ending up on our bill, she has reason.

14. *Did I Mention, He's Big?*

But soon Andy was speaking with very restrained enthusiasm about his time in the sack with Jay. My mantra being get beyond the *dick* to the *person,* I was undaunted, but another week and Andy was *begging* me to tell him how to get out.

"He's bright enough, Ned, but doesn't *read*—seems a point of *pride* with him. No interest in culture or politics, and he's not over Denny, either, whatever he's telling you."

I didn't like it—put the kibosh on Plan *"B"*—but what could I do? Kept to myself my conviction it was Jay's looks, or lack thereof, that lay at the bottom of Andy's discontent.

"If you're sure you want to dump him, I don't see the difficulty," I told him. "Act honestly on your feelings. Be straight with yourself, straight with Jay. No pretending, Andy, no sentimentality: Sentimentality's *false* feeling, and you must act according to *true* feeling. Anything else is cruel, and so's waiting until your feeling's pure vitriol. Whatever you dish out honestly and directly Jay can take, it's *pretending* that does the damage."

"I feel guilty."

"Why, when you haven't done anything wrong? If there's no future for the two of you, don't keep it your secret."

"What if he's crushed?"

"That's his lookout. Jay's a big boy. I know you resist this doctrine, Andy, but everybody's responsible for himself. If Jay has to take his lumps, at least they're grown-up lumps. Babying him wouldn't respect the man he is. Do I make myself clear. . .? Hello? *Hello!"*

"I'm here."

"You know, I'm a little surprised—"

"Turns out we don't have much in common."

"I thought you did, that's all. *Kids!* At least I'm here to pick up the pieces."

So Andy dumped Jay.

INVITED ANDY OVER for a Sunday evening post-mortem.

As he stepped out of Dolly's embrace and sat down with a drink, I said, "Guess who called? As if I had a plan: Jay's going to counsel with me at home."

Occasionally church counselees graduate to therapy at my place, at $50 an hour – so cheap because I lack official credentials (I merely know what I'm talking about, and how many licensed therapists can say that?).

"Of course he's a mess. Dumping him? And you've chased him right back to Denny, you know."

"Ned, if we'd met in a bar, a glance would have sufficed, we'd never have gotten together and no offense given. I feel bad."

"*Good.* Pain is to the point always, Andy – *never* not. Feeling pain's the healthiest thing you can *do,* lets you know you're *alive.* Which is more than you knew a few months ago."

"The lesson of a teenager, learned at 26!"

"Already some insight," I said. "But Jay will get over it, and meanwhile he's *blooded* you. And tell me honestly, don't you take some satisfaction in dumping him?" Did the waterworks threaten? "Andy, you wouldn't be *normal* if you didn't."

"Ned, all I want in life's a lover – "

"A romantic, forsooth! In search of that one man – one man only will do! – to be the love of your life, and so on and so forth *ad nauseum.* Makes me impatient, Andy, really it does, this romantic folderol some gays take over from the straights."

"All I want's a lover, but if I'm the unfeeling person Jay met, how will I ever find one?"

"Where did my matches get to?"

Deftly palmed them, carried them out to the sunroom and lighted up. My biggest bugaboo? Still self-pity.

Dolly trailed along and I put him outdoors. Noise was coming over the fence from the projects – "music" thumping like furniture being moved. Put on Tchaikovsky to drown it out; his blare of disillusion usually strikes the right note.

Somebody has to tell them the facts of life.

"Andy," I said, going back inside, "would you care to hear the scoop of my life on what I begin to doubt is the same planet as you?"

"Very much," he said, gripping his armrests as if he were strapped in and expecting the juice any minute.

"Then here's my *creed*: Every relationship between two people is best described in terms of *power*."

I paused to let it sink in. It's a heavy, not to say heady, truth.

"The secret to relationships – from my lips to your ears – is to establish a *balance* of power. Two people get together, *stay* together, because each wants to control the other. There's a quid pro quo, an exchange of – guess what? – *power*. Jay gave you too much, you gave him too little: Doomed from the get-go. You used him because he gave you the power to do so. You're only human. Believe me, that's no boast."

Dull resistance in those green eyes. Crossed his legs in defiance.

"Andy, in this world it's break hearts or be heartbroken. Every transaction between two people has a winner and a loser. Which do you want to be?"

He wasn't saying.

"Look, it's not a hostile world, only an indifferent one – one that takes a certain amount of guile to navigate. That's the way life *is*, and nobody has any right to be squeamish about it.

"You think to love someone you give your *all, all, all?* The less you end up with, the more it proves your *love, love, love? Wrong*. When you love somebody, you give your love. Meanwhile you have your work, your health, your *life* to watch out for.

"Work comes first: A man must do some one thing as though it *matters*. Work is serious, love amusing. Oh, love will accept any and all sacrifices without the blink of an eye—which is what they're worth.

"Now, you don't have to win *every* time. Sometimes submitting is more fun. That may be your way, in fact: With you, sex seems a way of telling someone you like him."

"I hate this," he stated, his foot coming down. "Ned, *love* is powerful, *love* is—"

"Earth to Andrew," I put in mildly. "If you want to *connect*, better play by the rules of the game. Power is *life*. When you don't have any? Guess what, you're *dead*. *Lamentable*, but that's the way it is."

Was he actually holding his breath? Bored, I got up to let Dolly in.

"OK, Andy, here's your lollipop," I said, returning. "You won't lose out. Look at you! Men are going to like you."

"I'm no beauty, Ned."

"No, practically speaking, you're *better:* an *attractive* man. Beauty's special. Beauty threatens, and no type's as universal as real attractiveness. *I* was a beauty—good for the man who wanted the dark man of mystery. Those who liked anything different? Had my work cut out. It was a limitation. You'll get the men you want. Question is, can you be trusted with this power?"

"I don't want it."

"Then put on your glasses, raid your closet, grow your beard." Lighting up, I kissed out a perfect smoke ring. First in years. Whence the inspiration? "But I think Jay could testify to your instinct for it."

"Jay taught me that good-looking people can do one thing more easily than plain people: Dump somebody. But where's the satisfaction?"

"In the *moment*," I answered. Kidding, but did he laugh? "Like comparing the pleasure of going *with* a guy to that of turning him down. The one – if you're *incredibly* lucky – lasts a lifetime. The other: *Forever.*"

"Ned!"

"Call me a cynic, but to the cynic belongs the spoils. Might I remind you that good looks are the original sell-by item? Spend them while you may. I'll keep my eyes open for you, but – "

"I know who I want."

Glanced at my watch. "I'm a little tired – "

"Mentioned him our first session, the kid at the Public Library? Oddly enough, he was staying in my building."

"Kismet! You know this guy's even gay?"

"Told him I'm queer, and he ran across the street."

"But you won't take the hint, will you? I suggest you scout out the frogs in more likely ponds."

Dolly gave up on us, started going round in circles on his bed.

"Ned, why is the paradigm of gay sex always promiscuous and anonymous? That seems so anti-erotic."

"*Anti-erotic?* You floor me! Someone existing as your sexual *object?* Believe me, everything's bigger, harder, more *lubricious.*"

"You mean knowing someone takes away from the pleasure of sex with him? Doesn't that imply you're ashamed of what you're doing?"

"There is no sex without shame," I delivered. "Nothing worth the name, anyway."

"How did you find Wayne? And know he was the one?"

"As for how we met, I'll tell you another time. But I knew our first night. Did I mention, he's big?"

Dolly sighed once and was out like a light.

"Hate to throw you out, Andy, but I'm tired."

Exhausted. Must be a saint, I really must.

15. *Stand Up and Sing for Joy*

STORY OF MY LIFE, reading the night away, everybody else arranged in hierarchical order in front of the TV crashing with *¡Spectaccolo del Domingo!,* each provided with a little glass of something (hers the smallest, necessitating a shuttle to the kitchen), when Mami calls, "*¡Eduardo! ¡Telefono!*"

Run out, untimely ripped from my room. Like to get these things over with.

"*¡Hola!*"

"*En inglés,*" hisses Mami in one ear, as a voice in the other says, "Hello, Edward?"

"Speaking!"

"Oh, hello," it goes. "This is Andrew? From East 10th?"

Everyone turns to look. Usually it's girls who call. Stretch the cord around the corner. "*Hey!* How's it going?"

"Fine, thanks, how are *you?*"

"*Great!*"

"Wondering if you'd like to see a movie or something?"

"Hold on." Mami's following the cord. Cover the receiver

and challenge, *"¿Que? ¿Que?"* until she retreats. "Know what, I'm in the middle of something, can I call you back?"

"Sure, my number is—"

"Better yet, be at the Library this week?"

"Every day."

"Good! Do it there!"

"OK, then."

*"See-*ya!"

Have to hang up in the living room, where everyone's waiting.

"¿Quién es?" asks Mami.

"Colega mío," I answer. *"De la biblotec."*

"¿Cuál es su nombre?"

"Andrew."

She frowns, rolling it around her mouth: *"An-drew."* What a doubtful sound she finds in it. Ten years in New York and no English! José snorts. Joselito looks from one to the other.

Me, I dive back into my room and pick up my book. But have the strangest thought: What does Andrew look like naked? Nags at me. Only one way to get rid of it. Salsa safely clattering, slip my shorts down and give myself a friendly hello.

It's great, but I feel disgusted even before I dab up with Kleenex.

NEXT DAY, I'M pushing the cart around the reading room, picking up books, when Andy-Tommy lifts his head and goes, "Movie?"

"Nothing good out," I say.

"Play?"

"Can't afford *plays."*

"I know a theatre, ten bucks, hardly more than a movie."

"Hate that amateur crap."

"No, The Human Condition Players? At Charas, around the

corner from me? Doing a Restoration comedy Friday, *The Relapse,* by Sir John Vanbrugh."

"What time?"

"Eight o'clock."

"Meet you there ten of."

What does it, the *"Sir"?* The hell am I thinking?

Go around about it, but decide I might as well show up. Nothing else planned. But if he insists on paying, I'll split in—what do they say on TV?—in a New York minute. Dutch is cool, friendly; being paid for, you know who's running the show.

No classes Friday, just eight hours straight at the Library. Get out at 6:00, cranky as hell, squeeze onto the express. Sardine can. Stand there and take it, hating it. At 72nd Street a Puerto Rican decks a white guy in a raincoat, sends him *flying* across the platform. Been feeling him up, he says in Spanish while the guy on the floor adjusts his chin, so the white people thin out fast and I get a seat. Catch the local at 96th. When I run in the door it's 6:40.

Wouldn't you know, Joselito's showering his blues away? About knock the door down. Mami comes out very concerned, I make my point about English majors and Restoration drama, Joselito jumps out and I jump in. Good shower, but brief.

Mami wants to know my plans, so to shut her up I open the phone book, shove Andrew's listing at her. She goes back to chopping cabbage—*savagely.* I keep running. Pull on fresh Calvin Klein underwear, gray Levi's and the Perry Ellis shirt Tia Luisa gave me for Christmas. Rush out the door at precisely 7:00, hair wet, jump on the One, change for the express, get off at 14th, *dash* for the L, for once am in luck, get to Charas at 7:48.

No Andrew.

It's an old school building falling to pieces. Nervous white people jam the lobby, looking back at their pretty cars parked up and down the block. Neighborhood types stretch out on the stoops in the balmy late March air, in no hurry.

No hurry indoors, either. Glance over a bulletin board of head shots mounted at cute angles—desperate smiles, skin texture of dead bodies. Creepy. Find a wall, put a foot back. Everyone's talking in that tricky Jersey accent about the best exit.

Then there's Andrew, spiffy in tweed. Actually I'm glad to see him. The house opens and people surge in. Forty, 50 people for 99 seats: They *run*.

"Sir John Vanbrugh's better known as an architect," Andrew says as we take our seats.

"Blenheim Palace? Hope he's a better playwright."

Love that startled look he gets.

Lights go down, everybody coughs, someone hisses, shapes scuffle past and—*pow!*—the stage lights come up and we're off.

Afterwards we let the Jerseyites charge out first.

"I'm sure you ate," Andrew says, "but if you like ice cream—?"

"I didn't eat. Like fried chicken? *Fantastic* Dominican place on 158th."

"Or pizza? Place over on Third has great Sicilian."

"OK."

We're to Second, the streets milling with crowds like a riot could break out any moment, when two whores accost us, manage to touch all the good parts. Mine says, "You're missing something good."

"He's *got* something good, if he only knew," goes Andrew, and looks like he can't believe he said it.

A cab stops short. Its hairy driver wearily flashes a badge and asks, "Those girls get anything?" We tell him no, and go in the restaurant. It's crowded.

"To go?" I suggest.

"My place?"

Duh. "One thing, just as soon not run into Veronica."

"Oh."

"Usually she's out by this time."

No sign of her, and soon we're there. Flip the TV on and sit on the couch. He sets the pizza between us.

Open a beer and grab a slice. "No cable?"

"Don't watch much."

"Good."

We see the last of a snowy Truffaut on Channel 13 – the betrayed wife training a shotgun on her husband – as we scarf down pizza and beer.

Asks if I want ice cream.

"Kidding? *Later.*"

Moves the pizza box, shifts closer. Suddenly there's a hand inside my arm, rubbing up and down! And he's going, "Edward, I really enjoyed seeing the play with you."

"Good play!"

"Don't know how you feel about me, but I like you a lot." Rub, rub, leans over and touches his mouth to mine! My ears roar.

Reader, we kiss *etc. etc.*

AT EARLIEST BLUE DAWN, the telephone rings and Mami says into the machine, *"¿Hola? ¿Está mi hijo Eduardo ahi? ¿Hola? ¿Hola, Eduardo?"* I wake up (still hard!) on the phone with her. What can I say? She loves me, and not every mom's going to track down her son in New York City at 5:00 in the morning. She didn't sleep a wink.

"We were talking about 18th-century architecture," I explain aggrievedly. "It got too late for the subway." Hang up, tell Andrew, "I better get going."

"Your mom? Glad you left a number."

"I must be psychic."

"Walk you to the train."

"There's light, I'll be OK." Turn down cabfare also. He opens the door. I close it. His lips burn! "Had a hot time. Don't call me, I'll call you. Thanks!"

"Thank *you,"* he says.

If Joselito wonders why I come creeping in with the first sun, he has the rare good grace not to say anything.

But I'm jumpy in my cot. Easier to sleep stretched out beside Andrew. His cock in my mouth made me feel safe for the first time in a long while. When I was a kid, Mami (we were living alone at the time) used to wake me up with a bottle of warm milk. My favorite time of day, safe at home before going out to face the bullies.

One day she goes, "*Casi diez años, consigue tu propria leche.*"

But why doesn't sucking a woman's breast make me feel that way? When Andrew pumps my arm, why does my cock stand up and sing for joy?

Oh my God.

16. *Boiling Over*

OH YES, ANDY-BOY hit the jackpot. Called Saturday just to give a cock's crow. Said the play had been surprisingly good.

"And afterwards?"

"Even better."

"You scored?"

Told me all about it: Two glorious blow jobs apiece, before mama barges in.

"That's odd," I remarked. "Usually Hispanics are into fucking."

"Oh, really?" he said in his tucking-away-information tone. "How big is he?"

"Ned!"

"Well?"

"My size. Thicker, maybe."

"Would I like him?"

"Ned!"

"Of course you used condoms?"

"No."

"When you *know* unprotected fellatio is on the CDC list—?"

"I'm not infected, and I'm sure—"

"Famous last words—*famous.* I'm *shocked.* You deliberately exposed yourself to the possibility this kid's semen has HIV. How *stupid* can you get?"

"Even the CDC calls it low risk, and I spat it out."

"Andy, though Alfred sounds—"

"*Edward.* Your namesake."

"—*sounds* like a decent boy, you ran a fatal risk in doing what you did."

"Next time—"

"*Next* time! Not seeing him *again,* are you?"

"Hope so."

"You're too new to get involved with *anyone,* Andy, much less a kid off the streets, and what with the disease aspect— Let me go, something's boiling over."

I meant me.

Don't know why I was so upset. That a newbie was getting sex, and I wasn't? Wayne had come over, but we had one of our boring arguments and broke up (again), and I didn't get laid, and doubted I ever would again.

NO SOONER WAS I home from church that Tuesday than Andy called, all excited, to tell me about making the discovery of the century at the Pierpont Morgan Library!

Said he'd justified his life on earth by sitting down for the first time at the Morgan to the original diaries of his Walter Terse, instead of working from transcripts or photocopies. (After Terse died J.P. Morgan bought up the diaries with indecent haste.)

Seems Terse every year bought a *Bowman's Court Guide* with dated blank pages which he filled with his daily entries, and Andy's earthshaking discovery was that he used the blotting paper bound *between* the pages to blot *other* pieces of writing, too.

Noticing slanting lines of mirror writing that didn't match the diary entries

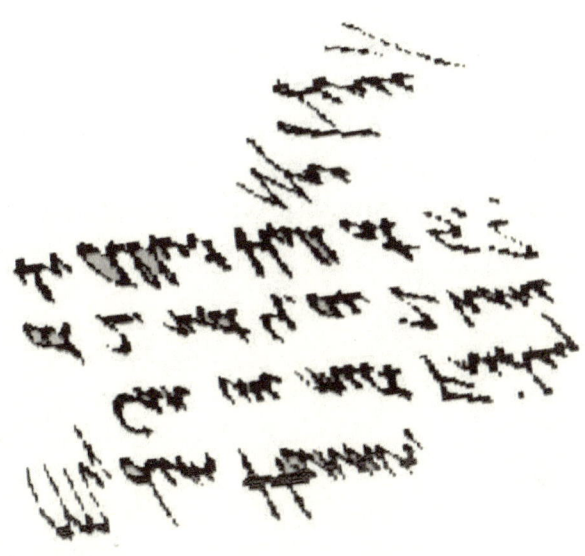

Andy borrowed her compact from the Morgan reading room's blushing supervisor and, using its mirror, turned the writing around and right side up and granted the world a brand-new Terse letter, thus:

> My dear Hannah,
> Can we meet Friday
> at 2, not 4, as I have
> to Albert Hall at 5?
> Yrs
> Terse

With more to come!

Clever of him, but—sucker though I am for lost manuscripts—it wasn't clear to me how this particularly enriched English literature. But every day that week he gave me urgent bulletins about finding more such fragments.

Great; *terrific;* but none of it was a bit of help with Plans *"A"* or *"B."*

17. *Unattainable Wish in Present Time*

OK, AFTER MY NIGHT with Andrew sleep late. Study all day. Sunday, too. Doesn't call.

Fine, told him not to.

But Monday, to work—and no Andrew. I think, OK, usually he's at the Library, but not always. Wish he was, is all.

Tuesday the same. Wednesday, Thursday.

What a relief! Between work and school, I don't have time for *anyone*. And who wants to be *gay?*

But what if the hard-on I get thinking of him points the way to go?

Hard-ons don't lie, do they?

What if the asshole's dumping *me?*

Bury myself in work and school like a monk. Alan compliments me, so I know I'm overdoing it.

Everyone keeps bugging me what's wrong, especially Akesha. One day she says that as my friend it's her duty to tell me rumors are going around. "That's nice," I tell her. "Appreciate it." Won't give her the satisfaction of asking *what* rumors. She does not open her mouth to me again.

Then on Friday Alan gets on my case. Heavy day in May, millions of students jamming the place to work on papers, which I have a few of coming due myself. When it's that busy, running around like chickens with their heads cut off doesn't do any good. I abstain, leave that to the girls. So when Alan lumbers upstairs to find the line winding out of sight, and me in the corner reviewing Dickens for five minutes, he goes ballistic.

Which, any way you look at it, doesn't help. As if the girls don't have enough to do, they stop to watch him chew me out. And I can't sit there without defending myself, right?

The word that gets him going? *Sissy*. Swear, I didn't know it packed a punch anymore. Thought it was like *pussy,* something everyone says.

Leave early. Walk home the whole way. Go up Fifth towards the park, and wouldn't you know, about 50th an old guy going the other way makes kissy sounds at me?

"You're *nuts!*" I yell.

That throws him. Takes him half a block to wing back his zinger: "And you're *not?*"

In front of the Plaza Hotel Tim Curry's shooting a movie. Scowls in that way celebs have of noticing *you* noticing *them (that* they don't miss) that makes them concentrate extra hard so you don't dare *speak*.

"Hey, Tim!" I yell. "How's it going, man?"

Not too good, judging by the look he gives me. (Ever notice how "celeb" sounds like a soluble fat?)

Finally reach the viaduct that carries Riverside Drive safe over Harlem. Ahead, northern Manhattan's stone-and-brick hill town. Over the hard gray water, Jersey. Look down, smack onto 125th Street. Gas stations. Kentucky Fried. In the distance blurry lavender projects. Clouds wipe out the sun, make the buildings look like tombstones.

That's when I decide to kill myself. Grab the railing and swing a leg over. Easy! Kids in a car yell *"Jump!"* and *"Just do it!"*

Then the fucking carillon lets loose. Fuck, the noise! Can't hear myself think! How can I do anything with all that *racket?* Glare at Riverside Church, catch the dome of Grant's Tomb. *Tomb?*

Splat! Can just see it. Beautiful corpse? Doubt there's any such thing.

Go home. Mami yells about the rust on my pants leg. Call Andrew's machine.

"Hi! It's Edward! Not around, huh. . . ? *Hmm. . . ?* Guess not!

Look, let's catch a movie! Call me! Haven't seen you all week! *See*-ya! Bye!"

On general principles give Joselito hell. A gloomier guy I never met, it's getting to me. Tell him he should make himself useful, do his share, at least go meet Tia Luisa.

Getting dark, try Andrew again, leave another message: "Listen, have a nice fucking life!"

And hang up. Amazing the punishment a telephone will take.

Put on my jacket.

"Eduardo, ¿a dónde vas?" Mami asks.

"Out to fucking kill myself!"

STORM DOWN Broadway so mad I see no one and nothing. Have a temper, I'm the first to admit; being Latino I'm volatile. So there I am, bumping into people and heading—no idea where.

"¡Hombre! ¡Hermano!"

What do you know! Here I thought Jaime was gunning for me, but he couldn't be sweeter. Miriam must not have let on.

"Hey, Jaime! How's your old lady?"

"Don't mention that bitch," he cautions.

"Hey, what happened?" Check how traffic stands, just in case.

"Come home last night and find her butt-naked with a guy"—he's breaking up, I'm about to offer sympathy, but he's not crying, he's *laughing*—"trying on underwear. How that whore loves lingerie! Half my money went for the Victoria's Secret! She goes 'Jaime, honey, how you like this G-string? Real zirconias.'" Now he gets serious. "And she wanted to bear my son? Fucking *believe* it?"

"Crazy slut," I console as we march through the valley and up towards Columbia. Pass four Barnard girls grimly pushing a dolly uphill. That dolly is *stacked* with boxes of birth control. I go, "Hey, girls, having a party?"

If looks could kill.

That lightens up Jaime, but I'm curious. "Who was the asshole?"

"Remember *Pablo?*" Spits it out. "Worse than if some mother was *doing* her. Told her, 'Want *this* 'stead of *me*, be my fucking guest.' And threw her shit out the window."

"So where's she staying?"

"Pablo's. She'll be back – hands and knees."

He wants revenge. I'm up for it. Suggest the G.W. Bridge station where pansy accountants catch their precious Jersey buses, but Jaime decides on Downtown instead. Hear a train, look back, see a southbound rumbling into the elevated stop at 125. "Oh *shit!*" we yell, take the escalator three steps at a time and, of course, miss the fucker.

But the next one we take to the end of the line, and I follow Jaime to the ferry terminal men's room. It's crowded.

"Are you *kidding?*" I say, and leave.

We walk around Wall Street – crooked little streets, *huge* buildings, *no one* around. Everywhere you look's a gothic cathedral 60 stories high, skyscrapers like Greek temples – banks in drag, I tell Jaime.

He says we should wait, catch one coming in for a shift. Buy some Heineken on his I.D., take it to a plaza overlooking empty streets, empty piers, empty river.

"Do some damage," Jaime says, hefting his first empty. It gets away from him and smashes into bits.

"Are you *crazy?*"

All I want is peace. Kill a few more. A tugboat rides past on foam. Much later, like an afterthought, its wake goes *slap!* at the wall. So I'm glad when a faggot hops up on the plaza like the White Rabbit and cuts across holding his attaché by a pinky. You can tell a mile away. That's what I hate about them.

"Hey, faggot!" I snarl.

He looks. They always do.

"Want to talk to you," says Jaime, snapping open his *knife!*

"You idiot," I go. "Put that fucking thing away! Want to get us in *trouble?"*

And so on, Jaime irate and that fag long gone.

This isn't getting us anywhere. Aim ourselves uptown, but at 14th Street I yell goodbye as the doors are closing. On the street the top of the Empire State winks out even as I glance at it.

End up at Veronica's.

Miriam's still there, and they're so glad to see me! Veronica loves an audience. She's rigged out in wig and makeup and cheaters. Also red heels—her trademark, don't you know. But what are they doing? Trying on bras and panties and negligees. Doesn't that get old? And man, are they high, I don't want to know what on. Hate that shit. Stick to beer from the fridge.

"You be the judge, Eddie," goes Veronica. "Which makes you hotter, black lace or pink satin? OK, here's me in black, see how slimming? Wait, don't decide—"

"Veronica, I can count every rib!" I tell her. "Dead give-away, women have the extra— Hey, you losing weight?"

Baritone: "No, I'm not." Soprano: "It's my diet, want to look *como un waif* like Kate Moss."

Miriam goes, "Jaime put on five pounds he *look* at a *cerveza.*"

That means beer, and it's not a nice thing to say. He can't help it.

"Shut up about my brother," I advise.

SO THAT'S HOW come I'm sitting on the stoop enjoying the scent of apple blossoms when Andrew gets home. As he's coming up the steps I go, "Get laid, man?"

"Edward! What kind of question is that?"

"Thought I was a mugger, didn't you? Really, really need to take a leak."

"Come up."

Piss like a racehorse.

"Dare I sit on the fatal couch?"

"Please do," he says, joining me. "It's good to see you. Been a busy week. Hoped you'd call. Are you drunk?"

"Few beers at Veronica's." Still have one in my hand.

"Oh? How is she?"

"Lots of new lingerie."

"Does she ever dress as a man?"

"Thinks she looks like nothing, jeans and a sweatshirt, but actually she's a cute guy. Plus you know what she's famous for?"

"What?"

I appraise my beer bottle. "Not that her shots can be doing it any good. Oh, look at your eyes get big."

"You mean she's *hung?*"

"Biggest in New York, Harvey Fierstein himself told her so. But she hates it, can you imagine? 'Course it's *too* big. Not like *yours."*

"Bitch."

"She's a bright kid, too. Well read. Believe she knows *The Picture of Dorian Gray* by heart? Plus any Ruth Draper you want."

"You've heard of Ruth Draper?"

"Aren't I supposed to?"

We're jammed together. Fingers start touching, rubbing, we kiss.

I go, "Bed?"

"Yes!"

He blows me, I blow him. Then we sit up, sheets lapping against our terraced abdomens while Andrew tells me about his big Terse discovery.

"God, you're brilliant," I go.

"No, no."

Says that, then hears coming from my chest Rice Krispies sounds he's never heard before.

"Oh shit," I *wheeze,* breathing short breaths that don't take. "Fucking asthma. Hear my bronchioles closing?"

"You OK?"

My focus is sliding off him. He picks up Volume One of Terse's *Diary* and for half an hour distracts me by showing me all its scholarly-editing apparatus, where his discovery of what he calls "superblottings" might fit in, and gradually my lungs loosen and I catch my breath.

"Fucking believe it? Left my inhaler at home."

"What sets it off?"

"You have roaches?"

"Yes."

Feel myself. "My erection's gone!"

"How flattering."

"Means there's more between us than just sex."

Close my eyes, he turns out the light, we snuggle in a puzzle of limbs.

"Sleep well, Edward."

"*Mmm.*" He's almost asleep when I whisper, "Andrew, I love. . . being with you."

"I love being with *you.*"

"I love. . . your body."

"I love *your* body."

"Andrew, I'm falling in love with you."

Suddenly he's the one can't breathe!

"Are you?" he says. "That's all right."

TAKE TIME OFF to study for finals.

Practically lock myself in Cohen Library. Know a quiet carrel on the fifth floor. My Greek grammar's open in front of me to the use of the aorist infinitive to express an unattainable wish in present time:

Ωθελε παρ–εναι
would that he were present

I wish.

Andrew's all I can think about, his elegant body curling into mine every which way, his beautiful cock. Suddenly I think: Erection's got to be the only word that in referring to the *state* of a thing means the thing *itself!*

Guess what I get?

Which makes it even harder to concentrate on how Greek expresses unattainable wishes. So when Tina taps me on the shoulder, I about hit the ceiling. She's in Nineteenth-Century Novel with me.

"Tina!"

"Eddie, you nervous or something?"

"No, no, not at all!"

"Foot's going like a rabbit."

"Always does that."

"Studying?"

"Like crazy."

"Me too, I'm so tense," she says, arching a hand to her neck and shaking her hair out of the way. "Stress bunches up, gives me headaches."

"Turn around," I go. "Here?"

"Umm."

Get both hands working. My massages are famous.

"That's good, Eddie, you got good hands. . . Eddie, you

know I got the key to a study room? If you want privacy, I mean."

"I'm good here."

"We could look at *Mill on the Floss,* you know I never finished."

Take my hands off. Not that I'm not tempted, but I think: This is for Andrew.

"Can't, Tina, exams coming up, got a shitload of work."

Gives me a steady, quiet look, accepting it.

"OK, Eddie, see you 'round. Thanks for the massage."

"Any time."

Drum my foot another five minutes to the thought of milking that bright taste out of Andrew, then go down to the phones, see if he's home and can I come over.

Leave a message, try Greek again. Then give up and go home.

Things are not so good there. Like everybody, Mami plays the numbers for a couple bucks a day. Christmas when she hits—once we had two weeks in Puerto Rico!—but a few bucks a day mounts up. She owes Carlos $11,000, and the vig on that keeps us dirt poor. Carlos has this man, Ivan, whose job is to collect. One ugly guy, Ivan, ever since his wife *(ex*-wife) shot him three times in the face. Not someone you want in your house, but what can you do?

Ivan's coming out the door when I arrive, so naturally everyone starts yelling at *me*. Mami shouts about laundry, José makes a federal case about the bathroom, even Joselito feels enough at home to complain that I snore, which in the first place isn't true, and in the second place, who the fuck's *he,* sneaking in from Argentina, taking *my* bed in *my* room and *complaining?*

I've had enough. Yell some choice words, stuff my backpack and go downtown to move in with Andrew.

18. *Real World*

PLAN *"A"* FINALLY got its boost. Andy presented his cornucopia of fragments to his boss, and to his *shock* found Professor Onorato unimpressed, uninterested and insistent that no time be wasted on them. Andy was staggered!

"Boo-hoo," I told him on the phone. "The finder of lost treasure given no *kudos!"*

"Ned, I'm the first to see that stuff, and it's been lying around a hundred years!"

"First, think how that makes him feel," I suggested. "Builds his *career* on the guy, *you* sit down to it once, tell him what he missed."

"Ah."

"And let me run it past you again: Here he's got this huge project steaming along, whipping *millions* of words into shape for – what, a dozen volumes?"

"Seventeen, projected."

"And he's up to volume – ?"

"Five."

"When you rush in and say, '*Stop the presses!*'"

"So forget the scholar's responsibility? Ignore the man's *words* – ?"

"Andy, welcome to the real world: Would if he could, but he *can't.*"

"He says I should publish them on my own."

"Is he making fun of you? Though I do smell a disser—"

"No! I'm through with academia."

"Someday you'll have to explain to me how scuttling along the baseboards of the 42nd Street Library beats being on the tenure track somewhere."

"Ned!"

"Here you thought you were mining a private Utopia, then wake up to find you were in the real world the whole time, but at a low hourly rate. Right?"

"Damn right," he said. "Living like a student, in practically a slum, because I believe in the Terse Project—but when I find a cache of new stuff, it's not the right *kind* of stuff?"

"The lesson here's the same you're learning sexually: It's time to grow up. *You* must behave as an adult, however new adulthood is to you. *You* must take responsibility for the work that you do—as well as for whom you go to bed with. Now, there are a lot of men—myself included—who *love* having sex with the lower orders—"

"Ned!"

"Sorry to shock you, but you say Alfred's Spanish—"

"Edward."

"—his mother's a cleaning lady, no father in the picture? Too easy! Don't think great sex settles every issue between you. I'm sure he's attractive, but you simply *cannot* know him as you must in order to express everything in *you* that deserves—"

"That's not true," came from somewhere off in space.

"It's no criticism of Alfred—"

"Edward."

"—Edward to point out that someone poor, minority and bastard *cannot* give Andrew Thomas the total support he needs from his lover. You have the time of your life in bed with him because you think it's free, but really it's anything *but*. And the harm you can do that kid without meaning to is simply *enormous.*"

Let it resonate.

"Andy, I have a young friend who's a researcher at ORBS Magazine. Loves it there, and he's headed places. His name's Thaddeus Switzer (yes, I know), and he's listed. He could help you find a *real* job. Hello? *Hello!*"

"Just may call him, Ned. Thanks.

"I keep pestering you to tell me about your novel. What's it about?"

"For me there's only one subject."

"Sex?"

"*Shame.* Not unrelated. I use class and status as a way to talk about shame."

"Gay?"

"No, sir, my book's deliberately *not* gay. My narrator's a young woman– Sure you want to hear?"

"Very much."

"Hold on, let me get some tea."

Put water on, let Dolly out, looked for my cigarettes. Hate the habit, but I'm a slave to it. Let Dolly in, poured my tea. Finally I was set. Talking about my book's a bore, but since it was practically done, I knew I had to face the music.

Told Andy all about it, or at least what I know (I merely wrote the thing). He listened attentively and asked, "How long have you been working on this book, Ned?"

"What is it, ten, eleven years?"

A silence, then, that I fully entered into. Talk about *shame.* Now he knew *me* better, had a handle to what ailed *me.*

"Professor Onorato's been working on Terse's diary for 30 years."

"Andy, that's the sweetest thing anyone's ever said to me!"

I hold an ironic vision of life, so sincerity cuts through me like a knife. What Andy said consummated our friendship.

"May I read it?"

"Yes, all right—soon as it's *done* done."

19. *Shut Up and Suck*

Do I get my big warm welcome? Quite the opposite.

"Tried calling," I tell him when he buzzes me in. "Busy signal. Don't you have call waiting?"

"No."

"Should get it."

"Actually, I'm still on the phone, about a job."

Hug him, whisper, "Let's go to bed."

"Let me finish my call?"

At last he's off, tells me about his boss's reaction to his discovery, how he's having lunch tomorrow about working at a magazine.

"Go for it." Me, I'd kill for that Terse job. Can imagine nothing finer. "Did I mention I want to spend the night?"

Seems better not to say I'm moving in.

"Great!"

Finally we get to bed. With that lighted-up look he teases my clothes off—makes me squirm with excitement. And vice versa. He's got a great body, not that working out would hurt it any.

Embarrassing how lovey-dovey I get when I'm close.

"My Andrew," I gasp, very shaky, "my *darling!*"

Even worse at *the* moment: "Andrew, I love you, I *love* you!"

Then we lie deliciously in each other's arms, exhausted, smooching like a couple of cats, sleep all tangled up. Whenever I drift towards waking, start to untangle, his heartbeat or breathing sinks me back to sleep.

Dream we're swimming, then realize it's the shower, it's morning and I have an amazing hard-on.

"Edward, get moving!"

"Do I *ha-ave* to?"

"We've got to get going."

"What's on the agenda?" I'm stalling.

He's tying his tie. "For me, the Morgan, moment it opens, because fuck Onorato, more Terse superblottings await. Lunch with this *ORBS* magazine guy, then back to the Morgan. But you've got work!"

"Com'ere," I go. "Missed a button."

It's a lie. Sweep the covers off and reach for him.

"Quick one," he says.

I push his head onto my cock. *"Umm."*

Twist up into his hot slick mouth, muss his damp hair.

Nice, but it's not doing it.

"Better if you take your clothes off."

"No time." Goes back to work.

Do my best, honest to God, but I drift farther and farther away.

"What's taking so long?"

"I don't know."

Think I'm getting closer when he snaps, "Edward, I've got things to *do*."

"Shhh," I say.

"I said a quick one—"

"Shut up and suck, Needle Nose."

That wipes his face clear. Stands up.

"Where did *that* come from?"

"Can't even make me come!" I say, pulling on my clothes. Fling my keys at the asshole, don't even deign to take a piss before I'm out the door. *Slam!*

I'd run downstairs, but Veronica's standing there in full regalia, smiling. Probably just in from a night's filth.

"*¡Hola, Eduardo!* A little spat? *¡Que lastima!*"

Go up to her. Sits down suddenly on a step. I never touch her.

"Mira, pendejo: ¡Una palabra y te rompo el hocico!"

"Hey, no hitting!"

Clump downstairs. Do I hear *"Edward!"* behind me? Or imagine it?

Go home, even if I should know better. Joselito's the only one there. When he says something about my coming back after all, I tap him on the shoulder. When he remonstrates, push him in the chest. Takes some silly steps backwards, but not another word does he say.

On to school, where—aorist infinitives and all—I ace that Greek motherfucker, and just like that my semester's over.

20. *Pablo*

I PULLED TOGETHER an ms. for Andy to read and called him. It was the day of his lunch with Thad, who'd already told me Andy'd be in like Flynn at *ORBS*.

Told Andy, "My sixth sense tells me you'll get this job at ORBS, and—"

"Knock on wood, Ned."

"My sixth sense is never wrong. But I have a favor to ask before you get it and are *immersed.*"

"Anything."

"Would you please read my novel?"

"Happy to!"

"Thank you very humbly. Tell me where to mail—"

"I could pick it up this evening."

In the background, shrilly: *"Aan*—drew!"

"That's not *Edward,* is it?"

"No. I'll see you later, Ned."

DOLLY GAVE HIM the full panoply of welcome, while I merely shoved a drink in his hand and said, "That's quite a hickey."

"Where?"

Directed him to the bathroom mirror. "What'll I *do?"* came his not-ungratified wail.

"It'll go away. But I *am* curious. Did Edward do that?"

"No. We broke up."

"What *happened?"*

"Sex turned into a fight this morning."

"Fast work, then."

Blushing, he told me all about it. Confirmed that lunch with Thad went well, though he said it made his afternoon reading Terse's diary at the PML seem futile, so he'd packed it in early and gone home.

Where, he said, there came a tap at his door. Through the spyhole he saw a cute kid.

"Who is it?" he called.

"Pablo. Eddie's friend?"

Opening the door, Andy said, "Sorry, didn't recognize you."

Short without heels, wearing jeans and a red sweater, Pablo looked male and appealing and *fresh.*

"Found this in my box," he said, holding up the Con Ed bill Andy never got for February.

"Thanks! Come in. Would you like something?"

"What do you have?"

"Beer, tea."

"Tea would be nice. You got a nice place."

"Thanks." Andy put water on, set out the mugs and found he was nervous. "Have a seat."

Pablo perched on the couch. Sitting down next to him, Andy was fascinated to perceive as masculine someone he'd previously only seen sashaying.

"You look so different this way," he offered.

"*Different,*" said Pablo. "When I put on a dress everyone says I look *great,* but like this they say *different.*"

"*Good* different," Andy told him. "You look *good.*" My God, he was flirting! Like sitting on the subway seeing a train pass and realizing *it's* not moving, *you* are.

"I think I'm ugly."

"Not at all. What's ugly about you?"

Bracing himself with a hand to Andy's knee, Pablo pointed to his face. "*This* is ugly, this and this, ugly lips like flat tires –"

Andy stopped him with a kiss and those flat tires filled. The kettle whistled and Pablo drew back, laughing.

"Go get the tea."

Andy got the tea, but no one drank it. Pablo scooted onto his lap and picked up where he left off, swiveling on his crotch and doing something near his ear that made him shiver.

"You come off so straight," he whispered, "but I *knew.*"

Andy worked his hands down Pablo's body. When he got into his pants and liberated what lived there he could only chortle. They moved to the bed, Andy marveling how he couldn't close his fingers around Pablo's cock.

Pablo whispered, "I like to be fist-fucked."

"I can't do that," said Andy, dismayed. "It's dangerous."

"It's *easy*." Held up Andy's fingers. "Short nails, even. *Made* for it."

"No, I'm sorry."

"Fuck me?"

"OK," said Andy, and took out a rubber.

"You don't have to, I'm clean."

"I'm sure, but let me," said Andy, and unscrewed his virgin tube of K-Y.

"I prefer Crisco."

"Crisco?"

"Don't you bake?"

It didn't work out so well. Andy kept slipping out—either his erection was betraying him, or Pablo was stretched out—and was nowhere near ready when, to a furious slapping of flesh, Pablo's body stiffened and convulsed. Andy withdrew (or slipped out) to find his latex erection daubed with feces and already shriveling.

"Yes!" concluded Pablo, turning to kiss him sloppily, Andy angling his body away. "We go crazy!" *Smooch!* "And think how *convenient!*"

I happened to telephone at that moment. Etiquette would have allowed the machine to take it, but Andy hopped over nonetheless.

"Aan—drew!" *etc.*

After I hung up Andy challenged Pablo, "I was on the telephone."

"Do you always wear your rubbers?"

He tossed it away.

"Now he's mad at me," said Pablo. "Guess I better go, huh?

I know when I'm not wanted."

"You don't have to–"

But Andy wasn't sorry to see him pull his sweater over his brown-nippled breasts, fling back his head and leave, this time flouncing.

After taking a long hot shower, he ended his day at my place, eyeing the stationery box in which was interred *Mixed Signals.*

"You must go for the Hispanics. Is he big?"

"As a matter of fact, Ned, *enormous.* Bigger around than a beer bottle, longer than–"

"*Too* big, you mean. That's as bad as too small and, believe me, if ever you land in bed with someone Nature was really mingy with, prepare for the most *blistering* critique of your performance, they're *impossible* to please. Your first fuck?"

"Yes."

"Why didn't you ever fuck Edward?"

"He never asked."

"You can suggest these things yourself, you know, or he could have fucked *you.*"

"No one's fucked me yet."

"You're saving it?" He blushed. "With Edward did you try frottage? Or the Princeton rub? Andy, there's a *world* of exploration you and he didn't even *glimpse.*"

"Think we should make up?"

"Certainly *not.* Number one, I *never* tell anyone what to do. Number two, you can do better. But the next one you're with, do some exploring. So two men in one day?"

"But didn't come with either one."

I touched the stationery box.

"Now, about this. The only opinion worth having is an honest one."

"Right–"

"Wait. I'd rather you hate it, shred it into *confetti,* but tell me *why*, than come back and say only that you *love* it."

"I understand," said Andy, reaching respectfully and taking my life into his hands.

"I know you do. Well, take your time."

"I'll be prompt. I'll get to it—"

"Not tonight."

"This weekend I'll read it through."

"Won't breathe till then."

"Ned, I want to say how grateful I am to you."

"Grateful to *me?* What *for?*"

"Everything. Most recently, this *ORBS* idea."

"Hasn't happened yet," I said. "But it will."

He sipped his Jack Daniel's.

"Tell me, what's the Princeton rub?"

21. *TIA LUISA LENDS A HAND*

FEEL GOOD AFTER my Greek exam, but I'm still mad at Andrew. What a faggot!

Get home. José's in the middle of the couch, hands on knees, magisterially watching a *Roseanne* rerun. Next to him Joselito sits dabbing at his jaw with ice in a washcloth. *Still?* Anyway, never touched his *jaw*.

Heading to my room when Mami comes to the kitchen door and says, *"Eduardo."*

"What?" The best defense *etc. etc.*

"Pablo me llamó al seminario."

"*So?* Hate that fucking pervert."

"Who call *who?*" roars José, on his feet and coming around the corner. "*¡Maricón cocksucker!*" Doesn't touch me – he knows, one touch, Mami walks – but backs me up with his belly.

"Dice que tienes novio," spits Mami.

A boyfriend! "That's not true." Say it so it registers. "Mami, on my immortal soul I swear that's *not* true. I'll *kill* that fucking bitch."

José gets his shrewd look. "Where you sleep last night?"

"Jaime's."

Joselito sees vengeance slipping away. "Papa, he hit me!"

"Dare you hit my son" *etc. etc.* LOUD. Can hear him in Jersey. Mami, wringing a dishtowel, adds her lament, while Joselito repeats his winner: *"Hit* me, Papa, he *hit* me!"

Noisy in there. Too much so.

"Shut up!" I suggest. "Will everyone PLEASE just SHUT the FUCK UP!"

No way. Joselito sucker-punches me, I reply in kind, Mami screams and José bellows, so I'm out the door. Which doubles the uproar, though even to me leaving home forever's getting a little tired.

"Hello, Eddie," says Suriya, sitting on the bottom step, demurely sipping her Colt 45.

One thing leads to another. She needs clothes, but DEA ribbons still festoon her mom's door and, more to the point, they changed the locks. So I break a window from the fire escape and pack her suitcase. Has to look fishy, but no one calls the cops. That's the great thing about New York, no one cares.

So I'm her hero as we go up to her new place in The Bronx.

THE BRONX IS not my favorite. Went to high school at J.F.K. one stop in, but never hung out. Where I grew up, in that Spanish slope of Harlem between Broadway and the river, you better know your way around – but The Bronx is *tough!*

Dragging Suriya's suitcase up her street, I'm thinking it's a nightmare. Buildings stick up out of fields of broken bricks like teeth in a grandmother's mouth. Suriya reminds me I said I'd marry her, and somewhere along the line I stop denying it. Need that roof over my head. So she's clapping her hands for joy – *engaged to be married!* – when we get to her building, where guys pour out, one waving a gun, but friendly. Suriya waves back.

Her place is a room not painted since Herbert Hoover, rotten planks for a floor, greasy range in one corner, dripping bathroom in the other, holes in every wall.

"We're home!" she says, and first thing wants loving.

"I'm not into it," I tell her. "You're pregnant."

"We can do it till it drops, I saw on *Ricki Lake*."

"Couldn't do that to you, Suriya. Carrying my child? You're a goddess to me!"

And more such bullshit. I'm grateful, *but*. She doesn't buy it, but when women think they have you down for the dotted line, they can be patient.

At first it works out OK. Suriya's so happy to be pregnant. Why do people have kids when they know what life is? Never understood, till I see how *happy* Suriya gets. During the day she keeps busy with baby stuff, hitting agencies to get on their lists and shopping for maternity things.

"Easier than shoes, even," she tells me, meaning how smart shoppers go shoe shopping in their stocking feet. "Look at maternity, you're *supposed* to be fat. Keep stuffing under, then ask where's the toilet, you're sick to your stomach, and head for the door. Stealing candy for a baby!"

Then we fight over whether it's a boy or a girl. Interestingly,

Tito's name comes up. Where's Tito, I go, he so crazy about her? She gets on to how I'm treating her with so much respect she wonders about my masculinity. Tell her to feel her fucking belly if she has doubts, or if she wants her last teeth knocked out, I can do that, too.

Men and women are so unsuited to each other, it's funny they even try.

THIS ISN'T GETTING me anywhere. Get to thinking about Jaime's floor. Go by his place, but he's moved.

So I visit Tia Luisa's Inwood district office. Should have done it long ago, I'm thinking as I tell the receptionist my name.

Tia Luisa is Mami's oldest friend, knows me since a child. She'll do anything for me, but sometimes wants it back other ways. Part of her front's poverty, to encourage the voters, so there I sit in a waiting-room chair with one short leg. I can make it rock, kind of, which annoys the losers waiting with that Ellis Island air of being fated to wait forever. Snapshots of folk-dance winners are taped to grimy walls, plus a photo of a wizened peach that says in crayon *Happy 100th, Mrs. Anita Perez!* and posters for the anti-drug plays they still make teenagers write.

How everybody hates me when Tia Luisa herself flings open the door!

"*¡Eduardo! ¡Mi amor!*" Squeezes the life out of me. "How are you, *¿muchacho?* Not about your Mami, is it? Come in, my son, come in."

She's wonderful. In her 50's, cushioned and warm anywhere you touch, a fat face Mami tells me used to be *gorgeous*. Her eyes still are – Ava Gardner eyes, very clear, very fast.

Takes me into her decrepit inner sanctum. "So happy to see you! Look good, but maybe a little tired."

"Finals."

"*Ach!* And your Library job I was happy to help you get?"

"Love it, Tia."

"Reading's so important! *¡Mira!*" Waves her rings at the literacy posters, old people reading to children. "But everyone's glued to the TV, *glued*. Speaking, your Mami still have that 19-inch?"

"Far as I know."

"'Cause there's a 36-inch fell off the truck, you and Jaime together should be able." She flicks a ring towards her storeroom, but recalls it fast. *"'Far as you know'?"*

"Moved out. That's why I'm here."

She listens with total absorption. It's flattering. Tell her about Suriya and The Bronx. She loves getting the dirt on people.

"Well, well: Little Eduardo. One thing I will advise, she sound so sweet and you both so happy, but take it from an old woman, don't let the honeymoon end in a wedding, *¿entende?"*

Tell her I do.

"Got too much on the ball to hand it over for pussy, pardon my French." She pulls out her drawer, finds the usual little boxes. "Listen, these are for you, and for her, how 'bout an abortion?"

"Thank you, Tia, I'll suggest it." Always with the cufflinks! My collection's already extensive, and when can I ever wear them? "But what I really want to know is where's Jaime? Lost touch, he moved."

She nods, doesn't say anything. Does an inventory of doors and windows. Just then someone passing raps on a pane, and in a split second she goes from serious to jolly, throwing kisses and shouting something I can't catch.

"What language is *that?"*

"Mandarin," she says. "You know the Chinese are moving in? Jaime's a fine young man. Sturdy. Loyal. But a little slow. Not like you."

Uh-oh.

"But this new thing he's helping with? Just goes shopping, takes his time, never a problem. Simple. But I can't send Jaime to the finer stores. A shame. If he looked at home at Paul Stuart. . . Used to be," she sighs, "with Visa, even American Express, all the time in the world, but *now!* In and out fast and one time only. Must be the computers."

"Wish I could help, Tia, but I'm working long shifts until the Latin/Greek Institute starts, then won't have a minute."

"*Latin/Greek Institute?* What's that?"

"City University holds it every summer? Honor to be accepted."

"Proud of you, Eduardo, so *intelligente* the way you study for success."

"I don't know, Tia, these days the smartest people are stupid."

"Truth to that, too, *muchacho.*" Writes something down. "Here's Jaime's address, I give it no strings, but in return– How much you make at the Library?"

"Up to 6.90 an hour soon."

"Do me a favor, ask Jaime he doing good or what. And give your Mami my love. Hey, and come up any time, get that 36-inch, plus" –smacks my shoulder– "*might* be a HBO box, her name on it."

I have to be fulsome. With us, though, no one's fooling anyone.

Everyone sneers as I come through the waiting room stuffing my pockets with cufflinks. Go straight down Broadway to Jaime's new place. Cell phones and Mr. Coffees are piled all over. He's so nice I'm on guard right away, though I go through the motions of asking can I crash.

"Stay *here?* With *me? You?*" he says. "Hear about Miriam?"

"No, thought you broke up! How's Miriam doing?"

"Got a new boyfriend."

"Hey, you were through with her, weren't you? *Shit!*"

"Yeah, I was done, but as part of the changeover to Bruno—"

"*Bruno?* Shitting me! What, seven feet tall?"

"Oh, you've met?"

"Get out of here!"

"As part of our little 'Fuck you, I'll get someone better,' she lets drop a word about *you, mi hermano.* About you and *her, mi amigo.* Ancient history that's news to *me.*"

Here goes nothing!

"Hey, Jaime, she came on to me, want to know the truth, I never *wanted*— I mean, of course I *wanted* to, she's a *babe,* but I never *meant*—"

Stands up, thinks tall and comes at me with remarks about my fucking his old lady while a guest in his home *etc. etc.* Which I can't refute.

So back to Suriya's.

FEW DAYS LATER get there hoping she won't be in for a while and won't be horny when she is. Outside two Dominicans are arguing. One walks off while the other crows unconstructive remarks. Their friends give them room. When I glance out the window I see the guy come back and lift a machete behind the other, who—*oh my God!*—is looking at *me* when that blade slices his head off! I get his last look—*so* surprised!—as he looses a curse so vile, it curls my hair! The neck gushes, body flops, head bounces on the floor and that's that.

Look it up, it was in *The Times* and *Daily News,* and the *Post* had the picture of the head back on the neck, face up. With the body face down.

No way I'm staying after that! Pack my pack and leave, don't *care* where. Seeing that head decapped? That's it for Edward and The Bronx!

Not like I let Suriya come back to an empty place. I wait, and during her maternity striptease tell her what happened. Damn mad she missed it, rushes out to look for blood. Don't they even wash the blood away anymore? Tells me it's collected in a signature gouged in the cement, ICE•E.

I split. I mean, she turned down Tia Luisa's abortion, very insulted: "What's that leave *me* with?"

Problem is where?

OK, downtown.

Take the local for time to think. Check my wallet. By some miracle I'm rich, $52, and there's a paycheck for me at the Library tomorrow. Means I can splurge. At 66th I jump off and get a room at the West Side Y. Thought Ys were cheap? But the tiny room's perfect: bed, desk, chair. I like things cut down to essentials.

Take a swim in a jewel case of a pool. Swimming's my sport. Shower first. Ten or twelve showerheads on either side, most in use. Several guys spend extra time washing their packages. One maybe has a hard-on, but you can't be sure because of his washcloth fan dance, all you know is it can't be much. Hunky guys, but I happen to think how much better Andrew looks naked than any of them and have to run! Near disaster.

Next day, buy breakfast, check out—meaning to check in at the monthly rate after I cash my check—and go to work.

Don't you know they fuck up my check? No check.

Do what I have to do. At closing time walk down to 3rd Street, sign in at the Men's Shelter. Going to be a writer so I have to do everything once. Also think, *What larks!*

Wrong. There *is* a hell and it's on 3rd Street. The jabber and threats of the crazies. The pitiful ancients whose flesh melts in folds that make you swear never to get old. The turds on the shower room floor. *Turds on the shower room floor?*

Know I won't be back before I fall asleep, my pack as my pillow. But no one warns me to sleep in my shoes. My Reeboks are gone in the night. In the morning I explode—like anyone cares. Thank God 8th Street still has the shoe stores with giant samples out front, though wingtips three sizes too large aren't what I had in mind. They give everyone a new nickname for me: *Bigfoot*.

AFTER THAT I'M really homeless. Not easy. Those reeking piles-of-shit-that-used-to-be-men who shuffle along, faces burned by alcohol or whatever? Hats off, gentlemen, respect for how they stay alive.

Sleep's the thing. Once upon a time, rumor has it, the Library stayed open all night. No more. So every evening I drag up to Central Park, browsing at Brentano's or Rizzoli on the way, sit on a bench as it gets dark and runners slap round and round, groaning. Running's more violent than I realized, lots of yelling about lanes. Watch the trees go gold, then black, skyscrapers blazing up like spaceships.

Once a brown car stops and a plainclothes calls over: "Hear any screams, few minutes ago?"

Then the runners run home and a new crew comes in like a shift change. Vacate my bench, no problem. These guys have syringes and things in their socks.

Find a patch of ivy under the wall at Central Park West that no one else wants. Rusticated stone at my back, trees drooping around me, no dogshit.

The first night I spread out my sweater, lie down and watch the moon rise like the crescents cut in awnings to let the wind through, tiny clouds of milk-washed blue riding brightly in from Jersey. Have to sleep light because it's still New York, and my stomach rumbles, and it's chilly, but I sleep the sleep of the just.

Next night's *cold*. May is not summer weather in New York. Luckily find a blanket in the ivy that's not too soggy. Rats and squirrels for company, and birds! Sunrise and sunset, the birds! Who knew they made such a racket? *Beautiful*. Fall asleep with arms crossed to hold in the music.

In fact, catch up on my sleep for the first time in, like, my life. My dreams are wild! Keep getting hung up on one about killing José. By the time dawn has me flopping back and forth for warmth, I've got a good rest under my belt. Cars start tearing around the curves, and I get out of there. Watch the city pull itself together for another day. Not a pretty sight. God must really hate us, and what did we ever do to Him?

When the Empire State starts glittering, show up at the Library.

What carries me through is my monster summertime shifts. Six days a week, eight hours a day – ten, Tuesdays and Thursdays. Plus the Library has showers, since working with books is the dirtiest job there is. The shower room belongs in a museum – green copper pipes, crackled yellow tile – but if I couldn't get a shower every day I'd kill myself for sure. Rinse my clothes out, too.

Alan loans me the $20 I ask for, bless him, so I can buy hot lunches. And when that goes, Akesha kicks in, though she hints she wants her money's worth. (Tell her I should bill her for services rendered.)

So day to day I get along, but something begins to crack. People at work start asking what's the matter. One night it rains and rains. Beautiful to see, gorgeous to hear, but unlike before it settles in and the trees give up, pour it on top of my head. No sleep. Don't see a soul all night except a few lost ones aiming for Columbus Circle and that subway corridor that gets so stinky on wet days. By dawn my skin's dissolved, I'm shivering and a voice distinctly says, "Edward, get off the streets or you'll *die.*"

But my late check and regular one come through the same day, I cash them, put money in each shoe – and they stay on my feet, I want you to know – pay back Alan and Akesha, buy a pair of argyle socks at Brooks Brothers (beautiful!) and move back to the Y. Live like a prince. Swim every day.

Someone tells me you can sometimes see Madonna dancing naked in her apartment across the street. Keep a lookout, but she never shows.

22. *Sadder Than AIDS*

ANDY TOOK FOREVER to read *Mixed Signals*. Finally, Saturday of Memorial Day weekend, he called up to say he *loved* it!

Of course he pleaded the excuse of his new job. Oh yes, in the middle of a recession, when every day you saw the zombie procession of the laid-off carrying cardboard boxes home, Andy got his fancy new job. But then he's the kind who always gets the job, the kind who goes through life with nothing too bad ever happening to him, blessed with health and smarts (to a degree), good looks (ditto), exempt from the shit that mires the rest of us.

For instance, one night he got mugged. What did it cost him? The 40 bucks in his wallet – in a neighborhood where people get killed for less. Don't have to worry about Andy-boy!

But then, most so kind as to read anything of yours take their lordly time of it. It's one of the ways you can get away with torturing someone. I'd do it myself, except I refuse to look at anyone's stuff (what's the use?).

Obviously Andy missed the whole point of the book, but the writer's meed is so often anguish that any prattle of praise is sweet. Invited him over to return the ms. and give me his thoughts.

While I waited my neighborhood was grooving to its warm-weather war-zone soundtrack. *My* block's tranquil as can be: Landmarked townhouses facing a 19th-century seminary standing in its own park. But years ago the city demolished the similar blocks to the south and built high-rise boxes, balconies wrapped in chain-link. It's the *noise* I find insufferable. Tonight some to-do had called forth a raft of police cruisers. Cops barking over their speakers sounded like dogs fighting. Noise begets noise until we're all insane.

Andy's arrival made for a diversion. After entombing the pages in my safe, I set him up in the wingchair with a Jack Daniel's, an adoring Dolly at his feet.

Had to admire my handiwork. Every time I saw him he looked more Manhattan. But whatever did I eat that made me so gassy? Of course I'm a pastmaster at the courtly art of the silent fart, but the smell (which I savor; everybody likes their own, in case you didn't know) meant poor Dolly began to come in for accusing looks.

"Andy, I am so grateful. Nothing helps a writer more than a good reader looking at his work and saying what he thinks, no holds barred."

There was a snap out my rear I couldn't suppress. But then, it's not healthy to.

He shifted uncomfortably. "I liked it," he said, "though I might suggest some changes."

"Tell me, what do you see as the theme? What comes across?"

"Shame, I think."

"Exactly!"

"You told me that yourself. You said you use status to talk about shame, but I didn't find that. Unless you mean her taking a factory job after Wellesley and lusting after a hunk there – ?"

"Yes? You slept with the son of a cleaning woman and missed that whole level?"

"Isn't that just snobby? And passé?"

Oops, another one got away from me.

"Well, did you get that it's her accepting that his origins turn her *on* that lets her get over her shame and go back to him? Not that it works out?"

"I suppose," he said. "I mean, sure."

Snaps issuing like a 4th of July finale, he casually brought his glass to his nostrils.

"I am so relieved, because my abiding fear is of being a bad artist. I sincerely believe it's a good book. For me, though, if it's not *great* I shouldn't bother. Don't look so worried: That question can't be answered in our lifetimes. For now I'll settle for *good.*"

"Ned, what do they make in that factory?"

"I don't know. Widgets. What's it matter?"

"It matters. I suggest you tell the reader what they make, how they make it and put Rod to work on the line."

"'The line'?"

"Assembly line?"

"*Hmm.* That may be perceptive. Let me think about that."

"Did you ever work in a factory?"

"Not really. Well, summer before college I slaved away in my uncle's big bakery. Had to feed this oven. Someone would wheel a stack of trays over, and every time a buzzer buzzed I'd shove one in. *Deadly.*"

"A bakery's perfect! Also – "

I interrupted with a whole terrific series. His politeness

fascinated me; not a word.

"Also?" I prompted.

"The beginning. If you start the book as Chlöe and Rod meet—"

"But the whole long story of how she ends *up* there?"

"*Um.* That could be cut."

Felt better after passing a thunderclap. Dolly woke up and trailed off to the sunroom.

"I'll certainly give the beginning another look. So tell me, why are you discussing literature with an old man on Saturday night?"

"Where's Wayne?" he countered.

"*Wayne?* Who he? Asking about *you.*"

"Ned, is it true we always kill the thing we love?"

"I'd hate to think *that.* Look, you and Edward had a fight, he walked out, it was all weeks ago."

"I really miss him. I was wrong. So stupid. Getting mugged somehow stripped some nonsense from me. He's just a kid. Nineteen! I have to cut him some slack—whatever slack he needs. I didn't really tell you about my mugging, did I?"

"That's OK, I know how scary—"

"I was headed out for two-for-one night at Sammy's? And at Tompkins Square there's a guy leaning against the fence, two others walking towards me deep in conversation, someone at the bus stop, then a shadow comes up behind me making crazy gestures and they converge. Stuck a .38 in my ribs."

"Oh my."

"Scrabble through my pockets, toss my keys and wallet—empty—into the asphalt, tell me to go pick them up. Do it expecting to be shot. Tell myself, 'These are the last thoughts I'll think.'"

"Terrible."

"Went by the police station, home for more cash and on to

Sammy's. Told a cute blond, 'An hour ago a .38 was stuck in my side.'"

"Not a bad line!"

"His eyes light up, soon we're at his place and I'm strapping his ass."

"Oh dear."

"Dreary indeed. But that's the bar scene." A few sips. "Ned, I don't mean to pry – "

"What do you want to know?"

"This," he said, gesturing inclusively. "How – ?"

"I'm not rich," I told him, "not by a long shot. My father left me a morsel, though you understand the Depression *ruined* my family. And several friends have kindly remembered me in their wills." Reached out and knocked on the table. (But what is this contempt for the dead that creeps over one in time? Couldn't they *take* it?)

"I so resent AIDS," Andy informed me.

"And just when was living not a matter of life and death? Know what's sadder than AIDS?"

"What?"

"The passing of *youth,* Andy! AIDS is just death, death, death – business as usual. Who said the most hopeful thing about humanity is that the newspaper prints obituaries every day? (Me, maybe?) No, wait until your *youth* starts to go."

"I'd love to see photographs of you as a young man."

"Sorry, but I'm Dorian Gray. My old photos have faded, crinkled, yellowed, turned red. So sorry."

23. *Moving In*

THE Y STARTS to get old. One day can't find my comb after my swim. Ask a guy can I use his? Looks at me like what he heard was, "Won't you please suck my Spick cock so you'll get AIDS and die?" Goes, *"No."* So does the next guy, and the next, till I get tired of my experiment. Besides, on my floor they're getting chummy. The knob starts turning late at night.

One afternoon at the Library I realize the guy in a beautiful blue suit next on line is Andrew.

Mind goes blank as he smiles. Very brusque I go, "What number?" and he says, "One seventy-two. I still want to apologize."

Doesn't register till I shove his books over.

"Yeah?"

"I tried calling."

"It was my fault," I go.

"No it was *not,*" he goes. "It was *mine.*"

"This isn't Terse stuff."

"I got that job."

"Hey, Bigfoot," says Miss-In-Your-Face Akesha.

So what makes me nod at the door? Andrew sets his books down on a table, hangs his jacket on a chair, says something to the next chair, walks out. Call downstairs: "On break, Alan," and walk off to: "Eduardo, it's not time for—"

"This way," I go, leading Andrew through the catalog room and down the south staircase. At the checkpoint I tell the old guy, "He's with me."

"Never been *here,*" Andrew says.

"Shhh."

Go down a hall, through another door, down more steps (most of the Library's underground) and into the boiler room, which I love. What a cave! Giant boilers line up like ICBMs. One's going for hot water, so it's not cool, but we're alone.

Soon I'm giving a cry of pure freedom. "Oh Andrew, I love you, I *love* you!"

Naturally as we leave someone sticks his ugly face in, heads for the boilers like he's on to something.

At most, the scent of sweat and semen.

Andrew insists I move in with him. Checks me out of the Y, gets me home, shows me the roach traps studding every undersurface, and says he stuck on each one as an offering against my asthma. He's so happy when I unpack my pack into a drawer cleared out just for me, happier still to wrap his arms around me, pull me over to the bed, start taking off my clothes.

24. *Pulling Out a Plum*

JUST IN CASE Andy was on to something, I gave *Mixed Signals* another look—and to my amazement cut the first *three* chapters!

Called him to read off my new opening paragraph. Didn't ask how the job was going; his moaning and groaning started his second week at *ORBS*, and I was tired of it.

"OK, here goes. Don't interrupt. 'Inherently dainty—'"

"OK," he said.

Was he listening? Cleared my throat and started over.

When I was through I gave myself a respectful moment—and picked up on something. "Andy, is someone there?"

"Yes—"

"Oh, your transvestite?"

"Edward? My friend from the Public Library? He's staying here."

"He moved in and you didn't *tell* me?" I said, injecting warmth into my voice. "When?"

"Week or so ago."

"Put him on. *Him* I want to meet."

A mumbled exchange, a voice saying, "Who *is* this guy? Don't *wanna.*" Then, blaring in my ear, very "on," "Hi, Ned! Edward here!"

"Hello, Edward, I hope you're treating my friend Andy well?"

"Trying."

"He's a handful, but he's a fine young man."

"Yeah? I'm two handfuls."

And so on. A natural flirt, and a telephonic tonic. Everything's in the voice. The face, yes; the body and its languages, by all means—but nothing adds a tittle of meaning to the voice, if only you listen. This boy's baritone was boiling over with youth and urgency and—all kinds of things.

Back with Andy, I said, "So far as I can judge without laying *eyes* on him, seems you pulled out a plum."

"He's a treasure."

"And my paragraph?"

"Ned, instant analysis isn't my forte—"

"Does it *grab* you? Your *gut* response."

"It's. . . *better,*" he said.

No rest for the artist.

25. *Bye-Bye, Luv*

"*Fort,*" I go when he hangs up.

"What?"

"You said instant analysis isn't your for-tay. It's pronounced *fort.*"

"No, it's not: *Forte*. Italian. Musical term."

"No, you used the French *forte,* meaning someone's strength or strong point. Don't worry about it, common mistake."

He consults his OED – retrieving it from the floor by my side of the bed – and finds I'm right.

Living together's OK. Everything's easier, and the nights are great. My body sizzles at his touch. Andrew says I *ground* him even if I'm *elusive* and he can't *grasp* me. (Suits me.) Still, frustrating that one goes first, the other follows. Try 69, but it doesn't work.

On Sunday afternoon we're knocking around that cramped bathroom. Going to Ned's later for drinks so he can meet me, but first Andrew wants me along to look at a studio for rent on West 16th. Needs a safer nabe, and is making the money to do it.

"Nah," I say. "It's for you."

"For *us.*"

"I can't pay the rent."

"Not asking you to. I love living with you. I don't want to get a place you don't like, that'll make you move out."

Fat chance.

"I'm so fat," I moan. Like to say it because it's so not true.

"Your ass *always* sticks out like that," he says, pinching.

"Don't!" I go.

"Don't!" he goes. "You'll get shaving cream – "

What of it? He's naked too. Before you know it we have to go to bed.

Just starting when screams cut through the airshaft. *Screams!* Andrew lifts my head, holds his at an angle, listening.

"Don't let's stop," I beg. "*Please* don't let's stop."

But so much for me! The screams move downstairs to *our* door, slap it shrieking bloody murder.

"*Aan* – drew!"

"What the fuck?"

"*Aan* – drew!"

"Let go," says Andrew.

"Don't open that door," I advise. I want no part of it.

But he's throwing on a robe, which means I have to scramble up, too. Opens the door, and in tumbles this creature in a sassy little sports outfit, skinny as hell, crying and carrying on.

"Pablo!" says Andrew. "What's the matter?"

"My *eye!* My *eye!* Doing my lashes and KrazyGlued my *eye!* I'm *blind!*"

Her face is screwed around her closed eye, but naturally the other one's wide open. Pull up my jeans before it hits me, but Veronica never did miss much. My luck not running into her runs out bigtime.

"Hi, Eddie." And she scans the stormy sheets.

"Oh dear," says Andrew.

Oh *dear?* Sits her down on our bed and takes a look. A black brushy thing bristles across an eyelid.

"Don't touch," I bark. "You'll get stuck."

"Do I *intrude?* Eddie, since when you steal my boyfriend back?"

I stop right there, one sock on, one sock off.

"*Oops!* You din' know. Me and my big mouth."

"What the fuck?" I inquire.

"Come on, Pablo," says Andrew, "I'll take you to the emer – "

"I said, What the *fuck?*"

"Once," says Andrew. "When we weren't speaking."

"Turn my back *one time,* and you—"

"He's *great,* Eddie, don' blame you being upset, we had *such* a good time—"

"No, we didn't," says Andrew.

Like I care. March over, find my clown shoes. No intention of ripping off the Nikes he gave me.

"Edward! Wait, let me explain—"

"My mistake," I say, cool and calm.

New screams from Veronica. She's beginning to fake it.

"We have Ned's later—"

"No, we don't," I say. "I can't make it."

"Look, I've got to get Pablo to the hospital—"

"*Hospital?*" she shrieks, suddenly sincere. Cups her hand over her eye and kicks like a two-year-old. Pathetic. "Not going to no fucking *hospital!* Just cut it off, I got more."

I'm all set. At the door I go, "She doesn't want to go to a hospital because they'll tell her she has AIDS and she doesn't want to hear it."

"*What?*" from Andrew, and a witch's cry from you-know-who. Kicks those gams!

"Hope it was worth *dying* for."

"Edward, *don't. Please* wait till I've taken care of this, then we'll go meet Ned."

"Who needs this shit?"

"Edward, since I got mugged, I realize—"

"*'I got mugged.'*"

"—what a *gift* every moment is."

"Who the fuck *cares?*"

I'm out of there. Veronica stops suffering long enough to say, "Bye-bye, luv."

26. *Fleetest Week of the Year*

ANDY PHONED from Bellevue to say they'd be late for drinks, but the caterwauling behind him made it an open line to hell, so I said another time would be better.

I forgot to mention Edward had called in fury to say that *he*, at least, couldn't make it later, not with *that* asshole.

Then how about right now?

Well, OK.

I love kids.

Arrived still in high dudgeon. Most becoming. I'd expected something along the lines of a Puerto Rican delivery boy, gold chain at the throat, vague growth under the chin. What showed up was something else: Tall, dark—*studly*. Mind you, he had his flaws (I always see the flaws first): Hairline a bit ragged, nostrils a touch ethnic. But a number regardless. A *dish*. Put together, *reeking* of sex, *hot*. Boys bloom in their season just as flowers do, make you long to bend over and sniff. And Dolly loved him right off.

"Come in," I said. "Down, Dolly! Doldrums, *off!*"

"Doldrums? How come?"

"Because that's where I dwell. So *you're* the one who's been torturing my friend Andy?"

"No friend of mine," he said—gruffly.

"Early for whiskey," I said. "How about a beer?"

That went over well. Installed him in the wingchair. I took the couch, crossed my legs, lighted up and caught myself shaking the match with an especially fey wave. Edward reduced me to a mass of nancy mannerisms. I love having a man around the house.

"You know it was the sight of you that changed Andy's life? Where was it, reading room of the Public Library?"

"When you got it, you got it," he said—sullenly.

"Tell me everything."

And he did. Did him good to get it off his chest. He calmed down, began to take in his surroundings. I'm sure he'd never seen such a room in his life, and that he liked it. It's a man's room, all right.

I flicked an ash. Certainly made a chainsmoker out of me. "Where are you staying tonight?"

"Not here."

"Definitely not," I said.

"Not at Andrew's. That prick."

"Well." I had to help. Often a third party can suggest solutions that elude those intimately involved. And relationships only grow stronger from solving their problems. "Don't you think it was good of Andy to help this person?"

"How do you help someone good as dead?"

"Where there's life—"

"—there's *shit*," he finished, acutely enough. "I was falling in love with the dipshit, can you believe it?"

"The ultimate humiliation," I said, "falling in love." His eyes blazed up in appreciation. "So for you it wasn't love at first sight?"

"Rome didn't fall in a day," he growled.

"Andy tell you he didn't have an orgasm with that he/she? That he lost his erection with her?"

Muscles letting go, his brow lost its shine. Not over him, whatever he thought.

"No."

"It's the truth. At that point he owed you *nothing*, but he didn't even have a good time at the hands of that professional seducer."

"Hands? Try cherry-red *claws."*

"Not *cherry* red? How common!"

Finally we shared a smile.

"Tell me, your feet can't be that big?"

Not a dirty-minded question. It was a Harvard professor of anthropology who made it his life's work to investigate the relation in size between a man's penis and other parts of his body, and it was his conclusion, after decades of loving research—mine but one of thousands of bodies he photographed after having his way with tape measure and calipers—that no correlation exists between penis size and foot size, finger size, nose size or any other kind of size.

"Size 11 feet, size 15 shoes," he said. "Know how shoe stores put out big samples so no one walks off in them? Didn't work. So you're a writer?"

"Finishing my novel." Started another cigarette.

"I'm going to be a writer."

"Yes? Hard life, you know," I remarked. "Everybody else lives more richly, while you're locked in your torture chamber. If you want to be *comfortable*—"

"Don't give a shit."

"Good, because—as I've had to inform more than one friend—the last words of an artist are 'I want to be comfortable.'"

"Your book a love story?"

"Yes."

"Unhappy?"

"Is there any other kind?"

"Can I read it?"

"You like novels?"

"Prefer memoirs, but not many make you think, 'This dude knows what he's talking about.'"

"Permit me, Edward: With your background, how do you come by literary interests?"

"No idea. Discovered I was literary in 9th grade when my teacher played the LP of Edith Sitwell reciting *Façade.* Like seeing my first giraffe. Gave it to my class perfectly."

Now the eye-rolling begins!

"*'Don't* touch *me, sir,*
Don't touch *me,' I say.*
'You'll tumble *my* straw*berries*
In*to the* hay.'"

I *laughed.*

"Ever live it down?"

"Not yet."

"With material like yours, you'll find your niche."

"Don't want a niche, want a pedestal."

"Did you know back then you were gay?"

Oh, deep silence!

"Do I know it yet?"

"Excuse me, you're straight?"

"Why not bi?"

"Unfortunate if true. Bisexuals seldom seem to build strong relationships."

"Did I use that word? *Relationship?"*

"I see."

Companionable sips of Heineken as his eyes roved amongst the pictures, shelves, *objets d'art* and veered round to mine.

"What causes it, anyway?"

"They used to say—Freud, anyone who gave it any thought—by distant, remote fathers. Then someone pointed out, hey, that's what fathers *are.*"

"I'm lucky, don't have one."

"Some say it's genetic, but that's only partly it, I think. A hundred genetic suggestions that life reinforces. Bottom line, it's perfectly natural."

"Do you like being gay?"

"Love it."

"Straight men don't understand."

"Straight men never will! I've often thought that men who go with women are a little like women themselves. The doors we open? They close 'em, lock 'em, nail 'em shut, paint 'em over, call it wrong and disgusting, and so on and so forth. *Talk* about it endlessly, as a matter of fact. (And they call *us* the love that won't shut up!)

"Conclusion: We must be a threat to straight men. But that can be only if they're *attracted* to us—if straight men maintain their sexual identity by dint of effort. Which makes no sense. I don't *try* to be gay, it's what I *am*. Isn't a straight man's identity just as firm? Or are they faking?"

"Yes," said Edward.

"Or is whatever *portion* of gay desire embedded in them so tempting it stays a red-hot issue? Most of us, you know, fall somewhere on the sexual continuum between all straight and all gay."

"Hmm!"

"So straight men are constantly disavowing their gay fractions. Look at gaybashers—*invariably* gay."

"What?"

"Bashing what they can't accept in themselves."

"But *gay*." He winced.

"You prefer—?"

"Lesbian!" His eyes sparkled. "I want to be a *lesbian*."

"No, no, lesbians are another kettle of fish entirely. Andy uses *queer*. I just can't."

"Or homo! Let's be *homos!"*

"I once proposed *joyiste*."

"I know: *Joyboy!"*

Eventually we settled down.

"My mom wants me to get married."

"Parents want grandchildren. That's natural, too. But whose life are you living?"

"What *is* a dipshit, anyway? Sounds terrible."

"I assume it derives from dipstick?"

He looked blank. Not every day do I get to instruct young men about automobile engines.

"In a car, Edward, one checks the oil by shoving the dipstick into the crankcase, then pulling it out and looking at it."

"For – ?"

"There you have me."

He drained his beer. "Show me your book? *Please?"*

He *killed* me. Eyes shone, teeth glistened, hair flew. How do you develop such charm in the slums?

"I'll read you the beginning," I said.

"Maybe I should have another beer?"

"In the fridge."

Went to the sunroom to find the new version. Out the corner of my eye saw Edward open a beer, pet Dolly, go along the wall looking at the pictures, then sit down and hoist up a leg, foot going a mile a minute.

Went back in.

"Not the final draft, you understand."

Cleared my throat and read. His foot paused in concentration until I was done. Then it resumed its Latin rhythm.

"Not so good, Ned, is it?"

I was amused. Criticism can't ruffle me. To be an artist you must be strong. "Don't think so?"

"You can do better."

"That I doubt. My talent may be thinner than I'd like, but that's why I hammer it out so fine: To make it *shine."* How he laughed! For a moment I got defensive. "Worse get published every day."

"You're using a woman's voice?"

"Yes."

"Too obvious. How long have you been at it?"

"What is it, six or eight years."

"Eight years!" He *roared!* "Fuck, I'm sorry! Ned, give it up! Good news: You're not an artist! You're free to go out and enjoy life!" He added, "*Sorry!*"

"No, no, Edward. Fortunately age and experience count for what they do. Will you stay for dinner?"

"What's to eat?"

"Listen to you. Cous-cous."

"*Cous-cous?*"

"From my year in Tangier."

A success. Fed him cous-cous and lamb without end. Outside, the light began to die. Announced I had to give Dolly his walk, and he asked if he could tag along. Glad of the company, I said.

Five sailors stood uncertainly on the corner of Ninth Avenue.

"My, my," I said. "Forgot it's Fleet Week."

"Fleetest week of the year," said Edward.

Fleet Week 1991 remains the gold standard. The Navy loosed on the streets of Manhattan 10,000 beautiful young heroes fresh from the Persian Gulf and not averse to people going up to thank them for their service (I did my share). And what queen designed that delectable uniform?

Dolly struck up an acquaintance with the best looking, but he just wanted to know where the Empire State Building was. We pointed to it—spraying a V of light above Chelsea, a hometown boy made good—and off they went.

So I ended up telling Edward my shipboard stories. Didn't mean to tell him my favorite (but I did), how crossing the Atlantic once I shared a second-class stateroom with a kid of 15 whose parents were in first. One of my queasier crossings and, desperate for a shower after three days in bed, I appealed for his help. Both of us naked, he helped me under the spray, I gave him a tweak and – Two things stick out in memory: He was big, and afterwards never said another word to me. Very peculiar. I mean, must have been attracted to me to get such a whopper.

From there I got to some of the real operators I've known, like Canon Sutter of the Cathedral of St. John the Divine, who for decades maintained a coterie of the most beauteous socially eligible young men in New York. Up they'd traipse to his baked-bean suppers and kneel to kiss his ring. What else they might have kissed I cannot attest, as his amusing table talk could never overcome my physical revulsion.

Edward loved it.

"Ned, how old was the oldest guy you ever did it with?"

"Let me think. Thirty-six?"

"Thirty-six!"

"But he didn't look it."

While Dolly pulled us back to the house, I was, to quote Milton (not usually my favorite poet), *"bedward ruminating."*

At the grating I quoted (not Milton), "'"Will you walk into my parlor?" said the spider to the fly.'"

Came in grinning.

27. *Drawing the Veil*

DARK WHEN WE get back and he pours me a Jack Daniel's. Need it. In that dust? Miss Havisham has nothing on Ned's place. Dust coats everything except the coasters our drinks are on. Creepy!

"Cheers," he goes, chinking my glass. "You know, Edward, you're what we used to call a real Erector Set."

Suck in my breath. "Ned! That's so dirty!"

"Simple truth." Sits there like a sylph in the wash of pink lamps that takes centuries off him.

"You're not so bad yourself," I say.

"If Andy could hear you."

"Fuck Andrew."

"You never have. In fact, a little bird tells me your sex life lacks variety. You make a religion of oral sex?"

"We lie there *wanting* each other – "

"How do you explain that?"

"'Cause he's not a woman. A cunt, you know, it grabs you, you have the bone to rub against."

"Fucking men is more spiritual."

"In the *asshole?*"

"Has it occurred to you you're both new to the game? I could help if you want."

Holds my eyes like I'm a wild animal. I stare back. It's fun.

"How?"

"Go to bed, see what you respond to."

Deep breath time.

"OK. OK, Ned, give me a minute."

Goes into the bathroom while I throw back that Jack Daniel's and belch Dolly out of his sleep.

Then we do it.

It's awful. I draw the veil. Try this and that, everything's dismal, nothing works. Wants to fuck me, but no way I'm letting him. Finally bring him off by hand because I can't bring myself to take it in my mouth. Says he enjoys it. Sucks and sucks, but the only way I can come is rubbing myself after he slathers me with goo. Weird, someone watching.

I go, "Was that as bad for you as it was for me?"

We have a good laugh about it. Says to relax with Andrew, do whatever my body wants.

"Wow, such wisdom. I'm going."

But Ned has like this ritual of smoking his stinking cigarette.

You know, the thing has set-up written all over it, which is one thing, but I'm supposed to lie there till he's done *smoking?* Fuck this shit, I'm thinking, when Dolly jumps up and starts licking Jergens off my cock.

"Don't!" I say, sweeping him to the floor. "That's *disgusting*—"

"Don't you hit my dog! Don't you dare hit Dolly!" *Hysterical!* "Edward, I must ask you to leave!"

Jam on my clothes while Ned lies there with big, scared eyes and, if you can believe it, a brand-new hard-on!

"He's a trained guard dog," he goes. "He'll attack anyone who threatens me. I have an alarm system."

"This is too fucking weird for me" *etc. etc.* Give Dolly a pat on the head—*"Bye, pooch!"*—and tramp back to Andrew's.

28. *Tiger by the Tail*

No doubt about it, Andy had a tiger by the tail—*and* his work cut out for him in the bed department: This one would take a *lot* of servicing.

But what a time I had! The reluctant, succulent delights of that primitive chemical factory between Edward's legs! But I always like the cock of someone I want, whereas that of someone I don't is the ugliest thing I ever saw.

Consulting my watch, I sat down in the sunroom and put on my thinking cap. Rain began to fall. In New York rain feels like commentary. From somewhere I heard that great blurry movie music of the '50s – speeding headlights spattering raindrops – while a new plan for publishing *Mixed Signals* suggested itself.

Why knock myself out getting Andy and Jay together when they weren't even friends anymore? Fine if Andy went into publishing; Plan *"A"* might still happen. But why not salvage Plan *"B"* for *Boyfriends* with a change of personnel?

Call it Plan *"C."*

Plan *"C"* for *Cubano.* Plan *"C"* for *¡Ay, Caramba!*

Of course, Jay Stern went for blonds, but it was safe to assume (if I know boys) that one gander at Edward and his stated preference would go by the boards. And Jay was free now. A few days earlier, thanking him for his help in becoming an independent person, Denny had moved into the SoHo loft of the owner of the gallery where he worked.

So Edward would net a boyfriend whose money and entrèe to publishing he'd appreciate, and a publishing career would exploit both his literary bent and his knowledge of the streets – he could plunder the ghetto for bestsellers without end. Give me time to polish *Mixed Signals,* too. That he didn't care for what he'd heard of it didn't faze me: Friendships work by *obligation.*

Plan *"C"* had the look of a keeper. But it was too early to bring Jay and Edward together; Jay on the rebound would do no one any good. Best keep Edward on tap at Andy's until the time was right.

Went in and dialed.

"Andy? Andy, hope I've done some good on your behalf. Edward just left, and if I don't miss my guess, he's wending his lonesome way back to you."

"My God, how'd you do it?"

"Talked things out thoroughly. You should do more of that. He's a bright kid: Don't hold back. Treat him as you would anyone at *ORBS*."

"I will!"

"He's one of those whose left lobe won't let his right lobe know what he's up to. If something's bothering him, he'll set off explosions on the other side of town. Pay close attention. Contrary to what people say, love is *not* blind, love needs the sharpest eyes *going*."

"You're right–"

"We went to bed to find things you can do together. Turns out he likes *lubricant*."

Heard him think *Hello?* And think it twice: *Hello?*

"Run that past me again, Ned?"

"It was just *sex*, Andy, nothing more. Wouldn't have done it if I thought you'd mind, but you both complain about being so bored in bed. . . Hello? *Hello!*"

"Ned, how *could* you?"

"Wasn't rape, you know, or magic either, and you're the one to benefit. Andy, if you're upset, I apologize."

Heard his buzzer ring.

"Have to go, Edward's here."

"Andy, first please say you forgive me."

"Goodbye, Ned."

29. *Cook-Pot Chorus*

"HEY," I GO, streaming rainwater.

"Ned just called."

"He tell you – ?"

"He's a jerk, Edward, a *bastard.* Edward, I'm sorry, please forgive me – "

"No, *I'm* sorry."

We hug and kiss and tear the clothes off each other and go at it furiously, bodies grinding as if to trade Edward for Andrew, Andrew for Edward, and finally – for the first time – with a riot of bedsprings and cries of freedom, we come at the same instant.

Old Mrs. Economides next door thumps the wall: Thump! Thump!

"Get used to it!" Andrew yells.

Thump! Thump! Thump! Thump!

We laugh and laugh. Catch our breath. I reach over.

"I'm in luck!"

We do it again, to another cook-pot chorus.

30. *Miss Pensive*

THE CALL I DREADED but long expected came on a June Monday at lunchtime.

Left word with Wayne, stuffed a bag and cabbed up to the Port Authority (I don't fly, and Amtrak was sold out). Bought my ticket to Chicago and climbed aboard the Greyhound after the horde scrambled ahead. And found every seat taken. Have to stand to Newark, the driver told me.

In New York it pays to make a scene. They found a seat for me after all.

As we crossed Jersey and darkness fell, more and more seats were empty.

The bus is sheer torture, of course. But this was the last bus trip of my life. That thought lent me patience.

What lent me amusement was the young lady across the aisle: A smallish blonde stiff in her seat, endlessly sighing out the window and heaving a top that, deep as it plunged, revealed no greater contour than a chesty man's. She went endlessly through the compartments of her bag: *Zip, zip, zip, zip, zip.* I dubbed her Miss Pensive.

Reading on a bus makes me ill, so I alternated between looking at the scenery and groping my way to the rear to sneak cigarettes in the toilet, until the driver made such a fuss about Federal law I didn't even have that, but just sat and thought about Mother. Two of a kind, always. Abetted me in everything; no one ever had the kind of support she gave me. Poor Dad couldn't keep up. He simply expired sometime after I finished school, and I'm not sure Mother or I really noticed.

But she'd been gaga for a long time. Last recognized me maybe three years ago, so living to 94 wasn't the triumph it sounded. At 88 she broke her hip tripping over the telephone cord. From the floor she called me with a terse command about her living will, which mandated that no extraordinary measures be used to keep her alive: "Tear it up!" she ordered. "Tear it up!"

Done, but from the hospital it was to a nursing home, with a hip that never mended right and incipient dementia, and then a stroke turned the face of the vainest woman who ever lived into a Picasso from a bad period. The rest was horrors.

Dinner came at Scranton or so, at a diner offering a choice of fried chicken or pepper steak. Assume the drivers still get kickbacks. But imagine my astonishment when Miss Pensive came back aboard: *She* was a *he*. Having changed a few articles of clothing, he was brisk and masculine in trim white pants, a nice bulge where it belonged. I felt lost. Kept a discreet vigil to see if I might detect the universal effect of a bus's motion on a young man's crotch. Couldn't be sure, however. Young men are adept at hiding it.

At Cleveland Miss Pensive dashed about with positively balletic attack, and afterwards slept, or tried to. Once a booted foot kicked mine across the aisle.

Somewhere in the blank that comes after Toledo, at one of those predawn rest stops beloved of bus drivers (though perhaps it's as well they get air and coffee so as not to plunge into a culvert), we pulled off the Interstate and the P.A. growled, "Twenty minutes!" The driver disappeared. I and three others got off, an Italian couple and Miss Pensive. They went inside the restaurant while I smoked in the chill. No light in the sky. A tractor-trailer pulled up in drawn-out hydraulic lament and its fat driver circled it, kicking at the tires with a passion, then tore himself open and peed at a hub.

Why does America's heartland feel so like the edge of the Earth? Flicked my butt away and went inside to find the men's room.

At the middle urinal, heedless of me, Miss Pensive stood stroking his personal length of manhood. He was at half mast. After I finished my business, I said, "Let me help."

We took it into a cubicle. Felt good to get my lips around one, have it probe my throat. Not my usual style, but I had a serious need just then. At the crucial moment I pulled off and he beat his white spurts into the john. Then he warmed (and astonished!) an old man's heart by doing the same for me. Got into it, too; in its effort his face looked noble. Swallowed, even.

Boarded again as gray light began to disclose cornfields. The driver surveyed her mirror.

"Everybody back?" she called. Dumb question, and sure enough as we pulled out the Italians sprinted out of the diner.

"There they are!" someone yelled. "They're running!"

"Shit," said the driver, braking. "*Told* them, twenty minutes."

My orgasm made me sleepy, but I pulled a copy of *How to Score Tonight* out of my bag to give Miss Pensive in gratitude (I'm the Johnny Appleseed of literature), though there has to be something wrong with a kid who sucks an old man's dick.

But he was gone—*vanished*. Searched the whole bus. For all I know he was an angel sent to comfort me in my hour of need.

CHECKED IN—still vibrating from the bus—at the Drake. Why not? For, though far secondary to the sheer *loss* in Mother's death, the fact was I'd inherit the dregs of Dad's estate. The family foundry closed, never to reopen, after the War, but even so, it meant something.

Mother was lying for visitation at a home in Winnetka. After a nap, took a taxi out. She looked clean and pretty and waxen, and not like anyone I ever met; did no better trying to relate to her effigy than with any other corpse. The dead? Don't know 'em! Sat at the back to get away from the smell of gladiolas.

A sad side of living so long that hadn't been brought home to me before was that her friends were all dead. I was alone until her lawyer looked in on his way home from the office. He assured me things were "in good order" and fled. I'd have had a lonely time of it if Cousin Hattie hadn't turned up.

"So ghastly, Ned. Hope they didn't tell you? That's the thing with Alzheimer's, you lose not only your memory, your personality, but functions like *swallowing*. They were feeding her breakfast, went down the wrong way, she choked. Rosie, the nurse's aide, told me about it. Have you met Rosie? Perhaps she'll be along.

"Well, they did everything, but she could *not* catch her breath, just *hoaanuu!* That's what Rosie says it sounded like: *Hoaanuu!* Lost consciousness, and you know they couldn't just let her go, they injected her heart and jammed tubes down her throat and started shocking her, got her bouncing like a Mexican jumping— Ned, you poor dear, are you all right?"

"Fine, thank you, Hattie."

"She looks so peaceful."

We were interrupted by a godawful wailing from the chapel next door, where sandbagged teenagers wept with their parents, everyone so wretched that pausing in Mother's doorway to peer across at her in her pink seemed to refresh them. Theirs was a closed casket. The wailing came from a girl strapped to a gurney they wheeled in for two minutes.

"No!" she screamed. "Johnny, *no! Johnny! Johnny!*"

Hard to take.

"Car crash," explained Hattie. "Into a tree after the prom. They were drinking. She lost a leg. Does it break your heart?"

Broke hers. Hattie started to cry, so tears were shed at Mother's wake.

At the funeral we were two (Rosie couldn't make it). The minister did his best with an account of heaven's golden arches welcoming Mother (really). Saw her into the ground at Graceland Cemetery, beneath Dad's sooty stone, and got out of there.

This time I lucked into a seat on Amtrak. Roared all night to New York. No angel manifested himself.

Arrived at palest early dawn. Scraps of paper were blowing down the deserted streets around Penn Station. How New York looks to you after an absence gauges how you like the place. I could only think, *What a dump.*

Got home feeling a million years old. Dolly was pleased to see me. No Wayne, but it took an hour to clean up his mess before I could tumble into bed to recruit the strength to face the rest of my life.

I'd failed in my solemn promise to Mother: to place in her hands one day a published novel of mine.

31. THOSE *PERSIANS*

LIFE'S LOOKING UP. *Amazing.* Except Mami's radar catches me, she calls every week, once comes out with, "*Ten cuidado del SIDA.*" *That* I could do without.

But Loisaida I love. When the schools let out it crawls with iridescent purple, green and blue creatures – robed graduates of kindergarten and elementary grades, so proud!

Summer's hell, but on hot days the Library's exactly where you want to be – deep marmoreal cool. The best day's before the summer solstice. Get out of work at 8:00, go to catch the One. Sunset coats everything gold. The chrome accents shooting up the Empire State Building (so phallic, how did they ever allow it?) glow red-hot against the sky. But what hits me is the sun sizzling downwards between the stripes of 42nd Street! I have a thing for maps so already know the street grid's off true, but not till that moment do I realize the streets make Manhattan a solar calendar! Worship the sun bleeding into Jersey and rush home to tell Andrew. Can't count how many times we make love that night. No one gets much sleep.

At the end of June the Latin/Greek Institute starts up in the CUNY Grad Center across from the Library. Take leave from work for the duration.

The Grad Center's super air-conditioned. Honor to be there. Took my Greek at City from Prof. Stern, the Institute's director (and my Latin from Prof. Drabkin). Six weeks of five-days-a-week seminars, 10:00 to 4:00, hour for lunch and *monster* assignments: Heaven!

First day there's coffee and bagels, and we sit around the table, 16 of us (and don't you know, no one ever sits in a different chair than the one taken by accident that morning? Try it once and everybody tenses up, and when the woman comes in she tells me to go sit in my own chair). We chat away. Everyone seems nice, though I'm the youngest and some are pretty old, and a few even teach Greek (frankly, they look it).

After coffee we do some round-robin sight-reading of an interesting passage from Herodotus on *The Origin of the Quarrel between the East and the West*. Herodotus is easy. I thought. When my turn comes I read with a better accent than any, "Ουτω μεν περσαι λεγουσι κενεστηαι χαι δια την Ελιου αλουσιν ευρ ισκουσι σφισι εουσαν την αρηεν της εκθης τες ες τουσ Ελληνας."

"*Good,*" says Prof. Stern. "Translate?"

"Out of Persia—*um*—forgetting to be born—"

Titters.

"It's an idiom, Edward: 'Speaking of the Persians. . .'"

"Speaking of the Persians—*those* Persians—and. . . Because? Of Ilium?"

"Look at the case. What's the case?"

"*Um*. Accusative?"

"Anyone?"

Everyone.

"And in order to take Trojan prisoners, they— *um*. They— *um*."

"Anyone?"

Everyone again. In other words, they eat my lunch.

Andrew can't get over it.

"Let's run drills," he says.

"You don't know the alphabet."

"Teach me?"

"*No*, Andrew. If I don't have it cold by now, drills won't do a fucking thing."

Zits *I* don't get. A sprinkling when I'm 15, but suddenly I'm a rose garden! Gross.

Andrew claims he doesn't mind. "Ned could recommend a dermatologist."

"Nah, Clearasil's fine."

"What brought it on?"

"I'll cut out the dairy."

"Maybe it's stress?"

"From *what?*"

"Me? Maybe?" he says.

"*No*, not you."

"I know I'm— Well, Ned says *insufferable*—"

"Fuck Ned, you're coming along."

"Maybe you're studying too hard."

"I always do that."

"Reminds me of what my mugging gave me—"

"*Gave?*"

"So much! Asked myself, Why aren't I angry? And it's because it gave me a way to feel the joy of *every moment*—"

"Yeah? My life's one big mugging from birth, and *I've* never learned any lesson like that. *You're* the one should see a doctor. *I* just need more action."

32. *The Carnage of Broken Hearts*

MOST AGGRAVATING SUMMER of my life. Mother's death. Legal business connected thereto. And *hot?*

Not to mention I turned 60. Let it pass without celebrating, save for an especially nice time in bed with Wayne. And the writer's nightmare: Half an inch away from finishing *Mixed Signals,* day by day I had less idea of what I was doing! Terror was kicking at my gut—unless it was a spastic colon? Please God above, let me squeeze out *Mixed Signals!*

Called Andy one evening, got his machine.

"Just me," I told it. "Not life-or-death to anyone else—"

He picked up.

"Ned, what is it?"

"Thought so. Andy, reworked the opening. Very quick."

But not even his encouragement helped. My book was going out of focus, my finishing touches botching it, turning it to *sludge!*

One blistering July evening, I went to the A&P to buy ice cream. The reason I go the extra block is because they let me bring Dolly inside. What I craved was not a gallon, not a half gallon, not a quart, not a pint: I craved a half-pint. Don't want to get fat!

I deserved a treat. At church the night before, I'd made the best suggestion I could to a virgin counselee and been met with laughter. My mood was still tender.

They used to sell half-pints.

"Sir, we don't sell half-pints," the shelver insisted. "Sir, you have to take your dog outside."

"No, Mr. Abner says it's all right."

"Sir, Mr. Abner doesn't work here anymore."

This shelver was of that scary shaven-headed breed, except I saw him one day when he'd missed his appointment with the razor: Baldy with a gray fringe. Not so fearsome.

"I *know* Häagen-Dazs makes half-pints."

"Sir, city law. I'm getting the manager."

I'm the victor of a million such exchanges. It's the price you pay for living in New York. New York will crush you unless you meet it on its own terms, teeth and claws at the ready. If you're not willing to make a scene, you've no right to be here.

So why the hell, as I stood surveying steaming tubs of strawberry, blueberry, *boysenberry*– Why the *hell* did I hear the other-worldly sound of crumpling plastic? And know I was going to pass out?

My heart started flailing. I breathed–*gasped*–but couldn't get air. Grasped the freezer's cold edge with both hands while Dolly whimpered, murk blotted my vision and *something*–something in no hurry at all, but not to be resisted–started pushing me backwards.

Death!

Here's how grotesque an artist is. Part of me thought, "How interesting!" The saner part screamed (silently) I CAN'T DIE UNTIL MY BOOK'S PUBLISHED!

Barely hanging on when the shelver, smirking with triumph, returned with a man in a smock. They both glared.

"Sir, are you OK?"

"No, I'm *not* OK," I said, and fell on my ass! Never unconscious—held on to that much—but *collapsed.* Dolly, bless him, went crazy yipping.

They helped me into the manager's tiny office, where walls pinned with bills of lading were supposed to instill in me the will to live, and brought water in a cup only just larger than what the dentist gives you. At least they didn't make me stoop at the drinking fountain, built for people in wheelchairs; last time I used it, my back went out.

"Can we call someone?" This they were eager to do.

Gave them Wayne's number, but no answer, the whore was out. Jay's beeper was no help, but they got Edward at Andy's, and 20 minutes later, adorable in cutoffs and a Socrates T-shirt, he ran in, pale and scared himself, but so comforting.

"Ned, what *happened?"*

"Don't know. I was shopping. Thank you for coming, Edward."

"How do you *feel?"*

"Better."

"Let's get you to St. *Vincent's!"*

"No, no, please take me home."

Made it on my own steam. Edward sat me down in my wingchair, wiped my face, administered brandy. Dolly settled down and went to sleep, so I knew I'd pulled through.

Had it figured out. Heart attack symptoms, but no heart attack? *Panic* attack. Dear God, spare me!

I moaned and groaned about getting so *old,* and look at *you,* so splendid in your verdant *youth*—

"So youth is verdant?" Edward said. "And age is inadvertent?"

That got some oxygen into me.

"You're supposed to be all broken out, but I don't see a single pimple."

"Cleared up after I dropped out. Took exactly five days."

"So how are things going?"

"Fine."

"I mean with Andy."

"Fine."

"Everything you dreamed of in a man?"

"He'll do."

"He's lucky to have you."

"Don't I know it."

"Does *he?"*

"Keep telling him."

"You'll try again next year?"

He smoldered. "Try? *Do* it. *If* I want to. Ned, those people? They were *desiccated."*

"Andy was very concerned. He – "

"Ned, *he* suggested I drop out! *Me!* I've never dropped out of anything in my life. You don't learn Greek by dropping out."

Tears were gathering! "I'm sure he meant well, Edward."

"My Greek went to *water,* I lost the first declension, the easiest conjugations – "

"Stress is most mysterious," I said gently. "Has it occurred to you it wasn't *Greek* that brought it on?"

"No idea *what,* then."

"Possibly being in a relationship you're not ready for? I mean, that would explain displacing resentment against your partner onto your own intellect."

Speak of the devil. The doorbell woke up Dolly, and Edward let in a worried-looking Andy.

"Found Edward's note. Ned, how do you feel?"

Told him the whole story. His suit was beautiful and I told him that, too, but kept to myself that I could see the half-moon cut of his underwear. Didn't he know with Italian suits only boxers will do? But then, you know you're an old fogey the day you see a young man walking down 57th Street in his skivvies and feel offended, though no one bats an eye (and at least the kid has the body to carry it off).

"Shouldn't we get you to a doctor?" said Andy.

"No, no, *no,* I'm fine."

"What flavor?"

"Flavor?"

"Ice cream."

"Couldn't decide. Something fruity. It's so hot."

"Back in a flash," he said, and left.

"So where's Wayne?" Edward asked.

"Where, indeed! That boy's in for such holy hell – !" Pulled a cigarette out of the pack and just held it. "You and Andy do make a handsome couple."

"Yeah, yeah, just like the couple on the wedding cake."

Said it with his sullen street look, sitting on the floor by Dolly's bed, scratching him behind an ear.

"I hope you use condoms."

"*Yes,* Ned. We're faithful anyway."

"I'm sure, Edward, but men are not faithful creatures. I remember when my best friend gave up sex at the first *whisper* of disease, back in 1980, a full year before the first *Times* article, he said – "

"Gave it *up?"*

"Said he had to, because you can't trust *anyone,* especially *yourself."*

"He's been celibate since *1980?"*

"Actually, he was one of the first to go. Ghastly." Pushed the cigarette into my lips.

"And ironic."

"Fate does go in for irony. Still run into his lover, they were together 20 years. Don't look surprised, often *open* relationships are the stable ones."

"Do you think the government invented AIDS?"

"Do they still say that? What do you think?"

"If anyone invented it, had to be a gay man."

"Hate to hear you say that. My *mission* is to lift the burden of self-hate—"

"Yeah, yeah."

"So how does Andy like his job?"

"Comes home exhausted."

"I wonder. When I met him I thought, with his literary interests, he must be a *publisher."* And Edward's eyes lighted up! Reached for my matches. "Publishing's a nice life—lunches, work with literate people. Start at the bottom, assistant editor for no money till you find a manuscript and shepherd it through. And it keeps every option open. If Andy ever wants to write, why, Toni Morrison was a top editor before—"

"Great idea," said Edward.

"Don't tell me, tell *Andy."*

"Great idea—for *me!"*

"You? I thought you wanted to be a writer— Oh, I *see."* Put down my matches, slotted the cigarette back into the pack. Just didn't appeal. "Have you met Andy's friend Jay Stern?"

"No."

"He could fill you in, maybe even pull a few strings. His dad's a publisher." Eyes took *fire.* "You've heard of Stern and Grudge?"

"I think so."

"Well, that's his father's name on the door. Though now I think of it, Jay and Andy might be out of touch. You'd like him, though. Smart as paint. Just got his M.D."

Didn't have the strength to read him my latest opening, but he looked it over silently.

"It's better," he said.

"I don't care about *better,* is it *good?"*

"Pretty good."

"You're not just saying that?"

"No," he said, holding my eyes. Who knows what his were saying?

"Changed my hero to look more like you."

"Naturally," he said. "Ned, why don't you have a dozen novels out? What *happened?*"

"Believe me, Edward, I know the sting of 'Physician, heal thyself.' Did my best. Made it my business to meet *everybody* when I came to New York after Harvard. Networked with the *best* of them—made friends with Carson McCullers, enemies with Truman Capote."

"What does *networking* have to do with *writing?*"

"You slay me! You'll find out. Believe me, it took a thousand betrayals to leave me what I am. Plus my wanderlust interfered, perhaps other lusts as well. My year in London, made friends with Stevie Smith and V.S. Pritchett—he said I was like a son to him. And Elizabeth Bowen! We wrote for years: 'Eddie' in *Death of the Heart* is the only literary character I could ever relate to. So don't feel sorry for me: If the life force decreed no novel until now, mine not to reason why."

I was serious, as Edward paid me the respect of realizing. The life force, after making a puppet out of me for decades, now had *me* working the strings overtime on Andy, Edward, Jay, *anyone* who could help get my book published. Staggering to contemplate. There *must* be a divine plan, its energies and transformations too complex for us to trace. *Has* to be.

"How can *I* meet people?"

"The trick's to be young and attractive," I told him. He smiled. "*Available* never hurts. Remember, kiddo: Luck goes to the young."

"Is that so?" he murmured, pleased.

"Now I'm a recluse. People must think I'm dead. Maybe

that'll change."

"When it's published?"

"And if—knock on wood—*if* it doesn't sink like a stone. If it does, it will rise again, I have full faith, but too late to do *me* any good."

"Won't Jay help?"

"No. He's protective of his dad."

"Give me his number?"

"*Jay's?* What, take me for a snake in the grass? Ask Andy."

"*My* first novel will be about *you,* Ned. You've been angling—"

"Too late, Edward! Get in line! I'm 'Jack' in *Breakfast Antiphonies*—"

"Don't know it."

"And in *First Fruits,* I'm 'Nat.'"

"Never heard of it."

"*Queen's Weather*?"

"Nope."

"'Louise'! Should have sued. Though even that's not as bad as that pack of lies David Westgate calls his memoirs. If you ever want to make an enemy for *life,* just refuse to go to bed with someone.

"Edward, I know you don't like what you've seen of my book, but you'll grow into it. By the time you're my age you'll cherish it, I promise you. I am *not* deceiving myself—that would be *pathetic. Mixed Signals* has a long life ahead of it, but that life cannot begin"—here I put fingers to my throat, for saying it somehow brought oblivion hovering—"until it sees *print.*"

Best I could do on the fly, but you have to seize your opportunities. He took it in with big, dark, trusting eyes, and I drew my first free breath all evening.

Dolly barked, and Edward let in Andy.

"Peach OK?" Andy asked.

"My favorite," I said. "Thank you so much."

"Edward, can you find bowls – ?"

"Yes, Mother."

In a minute we were spooning down ice cream. Delicious. Andy scooched close to Edward on the couch.

"So tell me, how are things going?"

"Wonderfully," said Andy, and I could see his joy well up as Edward smiled sweetly at him. "We're in love."

"Sex is good?"

"Coming along," said Edward.

"Hey!" said Andy. "Actually, it's *great.*"

"Ned, you should see his face *during*, looks like I'm torturing him. And he wakes up like a madman, hair crushed to the side."

"I think Andy's handsome, don't you?"

"*Very* – for 27," he said. Andy'd had a birthday, too. *"Kidding."*

"Edward's taught me – is teaching me – so much," said Andy. "You're my two teachers. Between you, I feel like I'm going through a rolling mill, being stamped and shaped into whatever I finally become."

"Huh?" said Eddie.

"And the job?"

Fatal hesitation. "A little dry, to tell the truth."

"You can make a change, you know."

"It occurs to me, Ned, that teaching was wrong for me when I was hiding in the closet, but now I realize I have a lot to share."

I was too done in to do anything but push my spoon into my mouth and make big eyes.

Edward rolled his.

"*Share,*" he said. "Why not *take* a little first?"

"How are things with Wayne?" Andy asked.

"We made up. We always do. Or did you know we broke up again? And how's the apartment search going?"

"Dante should devote a circle of hell to Manhattan apartment hunters. Everything's small and expensive. The worst is how the supers let me know *their* cut."

"Andy, be neither a fool nor a saint about bribing whomever you must." Edward nodded like crazy. "You cannot conceive the importance of having your own safe nest in this city."

"But the process is so manipulative, so degrading."

"Degrading? When manipulation's the stuff of *life?"*

"If I have to manipulate someone to get what I want," said Andy, flushing, "I don't want it."

"Can you hear yourself?" I asked. "Purely in a logical sense, you're not making any."

"New York, dude," Edward put in.

"It's disillusioning."

"If disillusion be the price of a nice one-bedroom –"

" – dot dot dot," Edward finished.

"You're right, Andy, of course you are, but you can be perfectly *right* and end up on the street. Remember, you're competing in the marketplace against human beings whose nature is to go for the main chance. In Nature if Coyote's too fastidious to kill Rabbit, Coyote dies. At every step of the foodchain there's a beautiful fulfillment. So be good to the supers."

"Some people delight in enforcing the world's harshness," he said. "But they're only following orders."

"Touché," I said. "I guess."

"Fathers," said Edward – to Andrew's surprise.

"A shame, too," I said. "There's no greater look of ease than a boy's in the company of his father. But papa always bungles it. Don't think I got along with mine!"

"There's carnage in breaking hearts," said Andy, standing up. "We better get going."

"Great title for a novel," I said. *"The Carnage of Broken Hearts."*

"Better yet, miniseries," said Edward. "Are you really OK, Ned?"

"I will survive. So grateful to you both."

Andy assured me the ice cream was in the freezer (I'd had my half-pint), and home they went.

33. *Buzz-Cut*

"SMALL," I GO out when Andrew shows me his new, empty apartment.

"They're all *small.*"

"Two people? Andrew, could I hang on to your place? Place to study."

"Can you swing the rent?"

"Oh, sure. You'll see, it'll be better."

"OK, I'll check if you can take over the lease."

"Why risk it? Let's do it casual."

His eyes light up. Younger than I am!

"OK," he says.

The new place is a tenement flat on West 54th near Ninth Avenue left vacant by the death of the lover of somebody in Andrew's office. Landlady's picky, he was told, but supposedly a tip to the super would work wonders.

So over he went—ten minute walk from the office—to meet the super, former first violinist of the Budapest Symphony, earning his living in the land of the free overseeing a Hell's

Kitchen tenement. It's like the East 10th place, except smaller, but the middle room has a loft bed. The exact rent the super doesn't know, but guesses it'll come in at about $1,000. A bargain!

Andrew tells him he likes it, casually mentions "*your* month's rent," and the super tells the owner his friend's interested.

Next day Andrew meets the 86-year-old landlady in the cellar office she shares with boilers beneath the high-rises she owns in Astoria. Her jaw relaxes when he mentions his Catholic schooling, but that doesn't mean she's happy. Penciling figures on the wall behind her desk, she bitterly announces, "Mr. Thomas, you have fallen into a tub of *butter!* Mr. Robbins lived there 22 *years!*"

Meaning the rent she can legally charge leaves it far below the market rate.

Sinks her head and raises her fists.

"*Jesus, Mary and Joseph!* A $1,500 apartment renting for $876.17. How will I *eat?* Don't want it painted, do you?"

Per the law? But she stops breathing until Andrew murmurs, "No, no." She inhales, and he signs the lease and a check that cleans him out.

THAT SATURDAY WE go to a party in Tribeca at Dana's and Fred's. Dana's another researcher at *ORBS*, lives with her banker boyfriend. Borrow a suit jacket from Andrew, though he says I'm overdressed, and insist we bring a bottle of *good* wine.

"They'll like a nice California," he says.

"French, or I stay home." For Mr. Cool, I'm sweating. He's nervous, too, which doesn't help.

We get there, rickety ride up a freight elevator. My first loft. Something else. Huge, with spotlights picking out walls Dana and Fred paid an actual tagger to mess up. Every Manhattan leftover not at the shore is there.

Dana walks around topless, nursing her brat, but no one's supposed to notice. The graffiti artist himself's there, too, smiling and shuffling in untied sneakers and backwards cap, sharp eyes going every which way, especially sidewise at Dana's boobs. Spits Spanish at me I pretend not to understand.

As they thank us for thc winc, a scuzzy-looking ORBSite makes a big entrance with his English Mastiff.

"Sorry we're late," he says. "Didn't want to bring the usual bottle of wine, wanted something *special*, had to look and look."

And holds out a salami! And the dog licks it! Which no one's supposed to notice, either. Dana, baby at her right tit, cradles the salami at her left–*that* you could paint. Then she cuts it up and puts it out in case people want to get sick.

I stick to Andrew. Thank God, signing that lease gives us something to talk about! Some say he's getting a deal, others that he should buy a place. *Hours* of co-ops *versus* condos *etc. etc.* Oh, and Central America–the starving peasants, don't you know. Also how all men are rapists. Andrew protests and Dana, changing tits, snidely says, "*You're* not a rapist, Andrew."

My job's to look good at Andrew's side, chat up whoever comes by. One woman mentions her husband's marvelous job.

"Where does he work?" I ask.

"Forty-Eighth and Third Avenue," she answers brightly.

An ORBS wife boasts about returning to law school, then turns to *me*, my mouth full of mushroom, and asks, "Are you at ORBS, too?"

Andrew answers for me. "He's not one of us," he says, writhing like Uriah Heep. "He's a student at City College and a page at the Public Library."

Naturally she recoils. "Just a page," I assure her, showing my teeth. "Not a whole book or anything." She drags her husband away. Still smiling, I ask Andrew, "Why'd you say *that?*"

"Your mouth was full."

"You said, 'He's my nigger friend.' How she took it."

"Oh!" He is so stupid. "I didn't mean—"

I go, "Later."

Thank Dana. Tell her I know some guys could clean that shit off her walls and ask if she's a C cup or a D. On the way home step into the all-night barbers at Astor Place and come out a new me. First buzz-cut of my life! Birthday present to myself. Twenty fucking years old!

Get to Andrew's. Someone's sleeping in the hall three steps from our door, curled up on top of rags. Filthy!

Give a little kick. "Hey! No sleeping!"

Picks himself up without a glance at me. Can read his mind: Four other floors.

Shit! "Veronica! Fuck you sleeping out here for?"

"Miriam—" She doesn't look or sound so good. Clears her throat. "Miriam threw me out. Bruno made her."

"Out of *your* apartment?" The same. Well, what can you do? "Can't sleep here. FYI, there's a shelter on Third Street you might try." Stands there wobbling. "And this is for calling Mami on me, scumbag!" Fake a slap upside her head, slam the door and go to bed.

WAKE UP, BLINKING, when Andrew gets in. "I'll put a blanket on the couch," he's saying.

Turn on the lamp, and he's standing there, roses in one arm, dying drag queen and her pink rags in the other.

"Get that thing out of here," I go.

"What happened to *you?* You look awful!"

"Glad you like it. Get her *out*."

"No," he says. Comes over while Veronica uses *our* bathroom! "Edward, I'm sorry about what I said, it was stupid and insensitive" *etc. etc.*, waving his bouquet. Tell him get those flowers away from me, never treat me like a woman, but OK, apology accepted. Veronica skitters down the wall to the front room. Andrew gives her a blanket, hangs up her dresses and tiptoes to bed.

I turn over and go back to sleep. Not having sex with that thing in the house.

It's getting light when I next stir, aware of the warmth snuggling into me. I go, *"Hmm,"* and get closer, until the rug smell of her wig wakes me up.

Jump a mile. *"Off!* Get her *off* of me! Get her *out* of here, Andrew!"

Andrew jumps up too, leaving Veronica alone in our bed.

"Pablo, this is not good," he says. "If you stay – "

"What *if?* Get her the *hell* out!"

She whimpers her way out – *with* Andy's blanket – and we change the sheets and I take a shower. Cannot close my eyes again. Still awake when the old lady sallies out with a broom.

"Shoo!" she goes. *"Shoo!* Ya can't sleep here, ya *bum*-ya!"

I know it's a broom, I can hear her sweeping the dirt downstairs.

LATER WE GO UP on the roof to work on our tans. Sun pours down like syrup. I am *sizzling*. Want to show Andrew how dark I can get. The usual Puerto Rican girls hang out a window next door. I refuse to translate their remarks.

He asks, "Can I touch your hair?" Pets it, says it's like velvet as the crotch of his shorts snaps to attention.

Thunk! And *thunk!*

We get over in time to see the last dog sailing out the window of an abandoned building and land – *thunk!* – near the others on the roof of the Flats Fixed garage. One wags its tail in the middle of a pool of blood.

"I'll call the cops," Andrew says.

"Too late," I note, and go back to work. Ignore the whimpering. Open my eyes against the crush of sunlight. Rocky white clouds blow across the sky. A big one shaped exactly like Manhattan Island comes cruising overhead! The Battery skims past, puts me in Wall Street's cool shadow. A minute later I'm in midtown's shade, then an oblong hole passes over and I'm sunning in Central Park! Drops me in Harlem, where the wind changes like a dream you get stuck in and the cloud gets flayed into scraps.

Then Andrew's back. "I called them," he says.

"Goodie for you."

"Edward—" he starts.

"Shut up," I go, closing my eyes.

"Edward—"

In his face: "Know what? I'm *sick* of it. Sick of *you,* New *York,* my stupid fucking *life,* and—and— Try to get away, I try and try and *can't,* fucking ghetto shit grabs me wherever I go."

"It's where you're from," he says. "We all come from someplace. What matters is—"

Stand up, tug at the towel, go, "Excuse me?"

Cram my stuff in my pack and, without saying another word, walk. Get downstairs and hug the building line, so if Andrew wants to see my ass one last time forever he's got to push his head out through the window gates.

WEST AND—THERE'S the rub. Its being Sunday doesn't help, the day New York—built for action—disintegrates. On Sunday people wander the streets in what they wear around the house. You see babies in strollers, absurd little dogs, couples kissing like it's Paris or something.

Walk 14th Street beneath *compadres* roosting on stepladders trying to maintain their macho while guarding plastic bargains. I'm homeless, but no one knows. Don't have the stench, the mahogany skin, the eyes assessing every trash can for returnables. *Yet.*

Wouldn't you know it, in the crosswalk at 8th Avenue a mound lies under a sheet and a woman's shoe peeks out from under a cab's broken headlight, while a cabbie in Bermuda shorts makes nice to cops who're probably telling him they have to ticket him, if not for killing a woman, at least for driving barefoot. Traffic honks like crazy.

OK, says Fate loud and clear, take the A train. Waste a token, because cops are standing there, too, and what's on the platform? A dead guy! On the floor under a rubber sheet, in a litter of torn medical packages. Excellent shoes stick out, my size. I'm tempted. A nice-looking woman goes in and out of hysterics, a cop holding her hands between his. When the tears spurt he kneads her dry again.

Who needs it? Back to the street, call Ned, tell him I'm in the neighborhood.

"Come on by if you want," he goes in his flat way.

His place is dark except for slants of sunshine that make the dust golden. Puts a beer in my hand, sits me down, says my haircut's a mistake, "but at least one that will grow out." Asks, "To what do I owe the honor?"

"Wanted to say goodbye."

"Going somewhere?"

It pops into my head.

"Up to Times Square. I'm enlisting in the Marines."

34. *Smallest of Any*

LOOKED LIKE A THUG, and angry, too.

I let him vent. First he went on about corpses clogging the streets.

"That's New York," I pointed out.

Then he told me about the dogs. That roused me, as it would any animal-lover.

Finally he got to what Andy said: "Not one of us." "You're from the ghetto."

Very disappointed in Andy-boy. Twice in twelve hours he puts Edward down, once in front of people he's anxious to impress. Not sure these things are forgivable. They go too deep, cut into the quick.

"I see, and happy birthday," I said. "Can't say I blame you, though myself I'd choose the French Foreign Legion. There remains but one fatal flaw to your plan."

Glared delightfully. *"What?"*

"Recruiting office is closed on Sunday."

"Fuck," he growled, but relaxed somewhat, too. That he believed me was the thing; I had no idea if it was closed or not. Probably Sunday's a prime day for shoveling slum kids into the services.

"You can't stay here—" I began.

"Did I ask?"

"No," I admitted. "And you're not going back to Andy's—?"

"Not if he crawls here on his hands and knees and *begs.*"

"Andy's *might* be out, then. Why not your mother's?"

Because he'd walked out on that life forever, they hated him, and it would put him back in the orbit of a girl he got pregnant.

"Edward, Edward, Edward."

"Ned, she's not even attractive!"

The authentic voice of 20 years old.

"What do you propose doing about her?"

"Her problem."

"City could make it yours."

"Not if they can't find me."

"Let me think. I do have a friend with a spare room." Jay had that second bedroom. "First let me call Andy. Go out in the garden."

"And do *what?*"

"Play with Dolly. He needs exercise."

Out he went, and in a minute was cavorting without a care in the world. Hoped he wouldn't tramp in any dog-do.

Sat down and dialed.

"Andy, how are you?"

"Terrible, Ned."

His tale squared with Edward's.

"Want my advice? Give him up. Call Edward a learning experience and move on. Look on him as having been lent to you."

Cocked my ear to listen. No, never! They'd gone through too much, were too close—and the sex was great, that had to mean something.

"All very well to *say* these things, Andy, but the proof's in the pudding. If people take Edward for your colleague, you set them straight. When he expresses the *touching* wish that with you he's in a better place, you shove him right back where he comes from. Your cracks about—"

Click.

"Hold on, Andrew, I have another call."

Click.

"Who *is* he? I have to *meet* him." This in the fairy accents of my next-door neighbor Gerald. Gerald photographs those youngsters who parade their thumping good health through the skin rags. The traffic next door always drove me crazy, so it was fun having the shoe on the other foot.

"Who's that, Gerald?"

"I think you *know,* Ned. Unless—*ooh!*—he's an *intruder?* Look in your garden, dear. I mean the romping dark prince."

"You like *him?* With that *haircut?"*

"Not his *hair* I want for lunch."

"He's a counselee, Gerald: Off limits."

"Does he *model?* Is he *big?* Or don't you *know?"*

"The smallest of any," I said.

"Liar."

"Gerald, I'm on the phone." *Click.* "Andy, as I was saying, time to say thanks for the memories and let him go. You have something bigger than any love affair you have to *fight* for."

"What's that?"

Square one!

"Your *career,* Andy. Hadn't meant to bring it up, but Thad Switzer tells me so far you're not the *wunderkind—"*

"That jerk!"

And more. So there was life left in him after all. Glad of that.

"Well, *I* have full confidence in you," I said. "The trick's to inspire it in *them.* It's sweat and tears, but the fight for your career comes first."

"Bullshit, Ned. Edward means more to me than that crummy job or anything else. I'm fighting, all right, count on that: Fighting for *Edward."*

There's a limit to what you can do. I never claim to understand what keeps any two people together. My rule of thumb is if a relationship can withstand choosing a movie to watch, it's got a shot at the ages.

Saw Gerald's head waggling atop our common fence as he handed a piece of paper across to Edward.

"Andy, hold on a minute? Someone here I want you to talk to, and then if I might have a final word."

Went to the sunroom, opened the door. *"Dolly!* Here, boy! Edward, someone on the phone for you. Wipe your feet."

Rebellion was limited to his eyes. Stayed where I was. Couldn't stand it.

Finally went in and caught the sappy last of it: "Never again, my love. . . Be right over. . . Or pastry at De Robertis? Hold on, Ned's here." Hugged me. "Wonder worker, thank you."

I took the phone.

"While I have you both, let me read my new paragraph."

Cleared my throat and gave it to them.

Andy said it was an improvement. Edward said I should hang it up right there.

"WHO'S THAT GERALD dude?" he asked after Andy rang off. "Says he wants to take my picture."

"He's a pornographer, Edward. He wants to shoot close-ups of your *dick.*"

"That's *disgusting!"*

"Mind you, he's good at what he does. Doing my jacket photo."

"A crotch shot for your cover? Ned, it'll kill sales!"

"No, smartie, my face. Like this." I balanced a weighty authorial head on two fingers. "Have I shown you his shots of Wayne?"

"No!" And he wasn't leaving till he saw the portfolio. But I love to whip it out. "Andrew thinks Wayne doesn't exist."

"That Andy. Beginning to wonder about *him*. I think you can see from these the photographic proof positive."

But he was disappointed. "Thought I was going to see his cock."

"The Speedo shows everything you need to see. There aren't any *au natural.*"

"Come on, *give.*"

"Believe me, Edward, he stayed covered the whole time. I was there, and I made him. Don't you see how beautiful his body is?"

"Not the handsomest," he said. "Looks dumb, too."

"Don't tell me about his *face*. The *body.*"

"Must live in the weight room."

"That he does—but where most of them wear their muscles over layers of fat, like someone poked a straw in their chest and *blew?* Not one ounce of fat to *Wayne's* muscles." Took the album and kissed it. "Male beauty," I lectured, "lies in the perfection of proportions. Wayne's the only man I know with *perfect* proportions."

"Proportions?"

"Edward, in and of itself the human body's gross. The proof is who can stand to see a—you know."

"What?"

"What you saw."

"Corpse?"

"Thank you. Only *proportion* can redeem flesh. But when a body's lean and every part in proper relation to every other, proportion invests it with that rarest of garments, *beauty.*"

Talking about Wayne's body makes me lyrical.

"He's *small*, that's why you won't—"

"Au contraire. As Mrs. Rock Hudson said about her husband, with Wayne everything is in proportion, thank you. *Everything.*"

35. *CROTCH SHOT*

HELL, I'M FLATTERED. I've seen those porn mags – perused them incredulously to see what faggots go for. Am I in that league? Think it over, but finally call that Gerald dude and say OK, but no nudes. He says fine, come by tomorrow.

Next afternoon leave the Library on a pretext. No point telling Andrew I'm getting my bod immortalized since if the pix turn out, I'll give him a set and I'm not going to have *sex*. What I do with my body's my business, not his, unless I have *sex*, and then it's only breaking a promise – not that I ever would.

So I dash to East 10th, do push-ups and crunches, shower, put my Speedo on beneath my jeans and go over. Luckily my hair still looks sexy. Just as glad not to run into Veronica or Ned.

Gerald's happy to see me. Glues his eyes between my legs, introduces his assistant – Chester, skinny, mustache – and takes me into his sunroom studio, cloths on floor and walls.

Picks up a clipboard.

"You *are* over 18, right?"

"Oh sure, 20."

"Sign this release and we're in business."

"Thought they'd be just for me?"

"No, no. See, I'm a freelance: I sell them, you get a modeling fee."

"You're *paying* me?"

"Sure, depending. Looking at you, I'd say *Blueboy*. Chest hair?"

"No."

"*Mandate*, too, then."

Don't know if I like what's going on. Tingling all over, tell the truth. But I sign.

"Eddie, why don't you stand over there?"

Chester snaps on the lights, I go where they're aimed, it goes from warm to hot in a hurry. Gerald ducks behind a tripod. Feel lonely. Try a smile.

"My dear, *where* did you get those big eyes?" he asks. Then pops up. "Oops! Forgot something. Take off your clothes."

Fine, down to my swimsuit. Suck in, flex, loosen up to the *Cars* tape that's playing. Kind of fun.

"You have a good body, dear, but they don't pay for Speedos."

"How much we talking?"

He shrugs.

Why not? What's the big deal?

"That's the spirit. Nice, *real* nice. No smiling, just glare—more *you*, dear. Natural poser, eh, Chet?"

Chet agrees. Gerald's camera goes purr, *snap!* purr, *snap!* and I start to get into it. Looking into that bright little lens is easy as looking in the mirror. Purr, *snap!*

Gerald pops up again.

"All right, dear, *good*. Now let's get it up."

"I wasn't thinking *erection*."

"C'mon, give us a nice big hard-on."

"Need help?" says Chet. And steps up and fluffs me!

It's very effective.

"I'm not the biggest," I apologize.

"Kidding, hon? Not bad at all, and with *my* angles?" Comes up, shoots from below. Purr, *snap!* "That's right, give us Sinatra. *Yes!* Bring that ass this way."

"Yes!" says Chet.

Purr, *snap!*

"OK, now take a seat."

Chet shoves a chair over and Gerald positions my leg across the arm. Gives me a tug, too, which I don't need or like.

"Lean back and grab yourself, thumb and finger. Show him, Chet." Chet shows me. "See, you're so big your fingers don't go around. Against your face, looks nine, ten easy. (Tricks of the trade, hon.) Now gimme face. Pout. *Nice!*"

I'm naked, hard as steel, under lights, a camera snapping, two guys devouring me, Gerald going, "Oh, good sneer!" Feel sick, but at the same time transported.

Purr, *snap!* What am I *doing?* Need air.

"Know what?" I go, standing up.

"Going soft? Chet."

"No, I have to go."

"John's in there."

"No more," I say. "Sorry."

"What's the matter, hon? We just started."

"Where're my clothes?"

"Eddie, this is not professional!"

"Damn right it's not."

It's humiliating, but while I'm looking for my clothes Chet grabs me from behind, Gerald crouches in front and—when someone's chewing your dick, better not struggle.

"Don't," I plead.

But he's damn good. Big wide mouth, steady moist stroke, Chet nuzzling my neck. The way your body betrays you. If I'm struggling, it's to make it last. Then I lose it and Gerald milks every drop. Chet lets go, shoves my clothes at me, I put them on and, very shaky, get out of there.

But not before grabbing the camera and whipping that film into the air.

"The *fuck?"* goes Gerald.

"Have a good one," I tell him.

Get home, and guess who's on the landing curled up in

Andrew's blanket? And stinking! There's a puddle next to her, worse in her panties, her breathing's terrible and I can't wake her up.

When you come down to it, we go way back. Call 911 for an ambulance, con them into letting me ride in back, see her installed in a hallway at Bellevue. I split, but she's better off getting fluids in her arm than lying on the stairs stinking up the place.

36. *New Wonder of the World*

CALLED EDWARD A few days before the move.

"Andy looking forward to it?"

"Says the rent's going to crush him."

"He's making plenty now."

"That's just it, says it locks him into a job he's starting to *hate*—"

"Put him on."

"Hey, Ned," said Andy.

"Andy, you're not *not speaking* to me, are you?"

"No, no, just busy."

"One suggestion: If you dislike research so much, you might reconsider publishing."

"Hmm!" he said, a lift to his voice.

"Have the background and the temperament, and it's a nice life."

"If I could even get a job."

"Doesn't OrbsCorp have a publishing arm?" I hinted.

"OrbsBooks!" he said.

"And Foster & Hatch, I believe? Might be more your cup of tea."

Plan *"A"* charged with new life (I hoped), I was back with Edward, trying to reassure him about this new wonder of the world, that he hadn't gotten it up for days—not since his photo shoot, in fact.

"*Any* number of reasons," I told him.

"Like what, for instance?"

"Like you're worried about your friend at Bellevue—"

"Whore's no friend of mine."

"Or guilt."

"Hmm?" Gathered Andy was nearby.

"Gerald?" So quiveringly angry as to verge on the ecstatic, Gerald had told me all about it.

"I don't think so," he said guardedly. "It's my right."

"*If* the other party to your relationship says it's OK."

"*I* say it's OK. Damn, it was fun. He's in the bathroom," he added parenthetically. "Should I tell him about Gerald?"

"Would you want him to tell you?"

"No. I don't know."

"Wait till you do know."

"'Edward, I love you so much,'" he mimicked. Had him dead on.

"Take a tip from an old man—"

"An old, old, *old* man."

"Enjoy your power—"

"No fear!"

"—but use it well. Being with Andy has advantages for you."

"Like *what?"*

"Like sex—*safe* sex—and a roof over your head."

"I'm keeping this place, meant to tell you."
"Oh? But if you want to build a solid rela—"
"Yeah, yeah," he said. "Have to go."
"And Dolly's calling me."
"Ned, I wish you'd give your dog a boy name."

37. *The Clap*

My own place! I'm like Ned. He *can't* sleep with anyone; I can, but prefer not to. Sleeping's hard enough, takes all *my* concentration. Having someone breathe in my ear or wing an elbow into me? It gets old. Love the very word *apart-ment*.

If we tell the landlord Andrew's moving out and I'm moving in, he would, number one, slap on more rent—which wouldn't do me a bit of good—and probably refuse to rent to me at all for whatever trumped-up reasons. Our solution is I'll pay Andrew, and he'll mail in his check as usual. Foolproof.

Moving day this guy Jeff gets his beat-up van there after lunch. First he hires some kids to watch it, then helps us lug boxes downstairs. Halfway through the job I take a leak.

¡Ay, caramba! Who poured acid down my dick? *Burns!* Before I'm finished I'm practically crying!

What the *fuck*—?

Tell Andrew I need Life-Savers, brush off Jeff's, "Like Wintergreen, I got some," and go to the corner. Call Ned.

"Sounds like you picked something up from your escapade the other day."

Something cold grabs me! *"AIDS?"*

"No, Edward, yours is the classic symptom of something a lot more honorable: The clap."

"That queen gave me the *clap?* Going *down* on me?"

"Gerald eats penicillin like candy, he gets gonorrhea of the throat so often. With what *he* does?"

"I'll kill the fucker!"

"Calm down, Edward, perfectly curable. Let's see, there's the municipal VD place here on Ninth Avenue – "

"No way!"

"Wait, have an idea: My M.D. friend? It's his evening at the clinic next to Presbyterian."

"I know the place!"

"Meanwhile be thinking how you're going to tell Andy. Don't worry, he'll be supportive."

"Not telling him."

"Oh, that's right, you've been impotent."

"Got over it last night."

"Then he'd better see a doctor, too."

"He'll kill me!"

"You wish. And ask him to call me later."

Get my chance on our last sweep upstairs.

"Wish I were leaving you a better place," Andrew says. "And more furniture."

"Don't worry about it, I'm thrilled," I go. "Andrew, we have to talk."

"Jeff's waiting."

"Promise you won't hit me?"

"Of course not. I mean, I promise."

"I'm going to the doctor's later. I might have gonorrhea."

He's stunned! *"How?"*

How do you think, Einstein?

"I did a thing. With a guy."

His fingers go cold! "Unprotected?"

"He sucked me off."

"What guy?"

"No one you know, and I'm not seeing him again, except," I amend, "calling up to say, 'Hey, asshole, know you have a *disease?*'"

Quiet. Very quiet. "Edward, in this day and age, you have to tell me–"

"I'm sorry, Andrew. Hit me if you want."

The arms wrap around me! "That's all I care about, that you're sorry."

"You have such a sissy voice." He recoils. "I mean, I *like* it. It's hollow. Sexy."

"Do you still want to be faithful?"

"Yes, but I don't like rules."

"I agree, it should be a free gift." Jeff honks. "Need money for the doctor?"

"Don't know."

Presses $50 on me.

As we pull out Andrew says, "Already I see this block through uptown, careerist, 'Believe-I-ever-lived-*here?*' eyes. Kind of sorry you're staying on, Edward."

"Knew it! Changing your mind!"

"No, no, just–you deserve better."

"So true."

We cruise across Avenue B.

"Holy crap!" yells Jeff, rocking the van to a halt at the Carnegie library.

A crowd's pointing up to a hammock hanging from a tenement fire escape. A body's on the floor, one white marble foot sticking out from under a floral sheet–deadest thing I ever saw, and I'm practically a native New Yorker.

Helpful guy on the sidewalk tells us how his young actor

neighbor, wanting some rays, hooks one end of his hammock to the fire escape, the other to an eye-bolt in the brick, climbs in and enjoys the sun until his weight pulls out the bolt and drops him on his head.

New York has to be the world capital of grotesque ways to die.

"Let's go," says Andrew. "Drive on."

His peremptory command ruins Jeff's day. We have to do the unloading ourselves.

When I leave for the doctor's after a day of hauling stuff, I tell Andrew, "Ned wants you to call him."

Plugs in his phone and dials.

38. *Eviction*

"ANDY, SO GLAD you called," I said. "I'm sick!"

"What can I do?"

"I'll pull through – *has* to be a one-day bug – but I've got *church* tonight! Must be *exhausted*, I'm ashamed to ask, but could you *possibly* fill in?"

"Think I'm *capable?*"

"I have every confidence."

"Sure!"

"Thank you so much. The first hour was blank when I called Harry just now. At 9:00's a young man I saw last week named Charlie. Be yourself – sympathetic and warm – and you'll do no harm. Charlie's worried he's attracted to the S&M scene. Tell him about the satisfaction you find in building a relationship."

"Do my best, Ned."

Not one word about that wicked Edward.

What really made me ill was the previous Tuesday, when the Rev. Albright asked me to come in "for a little chat."

How these urban parishes maintain their old splendor, I wouldn't know. Father Albright greeted me at his study door, sat me down, offered sherry. One beautiful room. Carved walnut paneling. My God, that's a Saint-Gaudens plaque on the wall! And surely the lamps and windows are Tiffany?

Had his lines down pat and kept a smile on his bluff, handsome features. He *thrives,* sawing away at redemption day and night.

I knew exactly what was coming.

". . . so *many* needs, Ned, competing for such *limited* space. Can't tell you how *sorry* I am."

"But who would *want* our dinky little room, Father? Fine for *us,* but– Don't tell me it's the battered *women?* With that *empire* of theirs upstairs?"

"No, Ned, it's the parolees. *Enormous* needs. What you might do is move Gays Reaching Out over to the Lesbian and Gay Center."

"And how many coming-outers will head for Queer Central first thing, do you think? So *many* men respond only to one-on-one. A church is *perfect* for us."

He smiled beatifically. *Who squealed?*

"I hope no one's *complained,"* I said, "because heaven knows there's nothing to *complain* about. We're quiet, *never* fill up the lobby, pay for the telephone. I *personally* see to the trash."

"Not a matter – " he began.

"Cliff, we've been here, what, twelve years already? I'm nothing but grateful to *you,* but while things have *improved* for gay people, I assure you we *still*—"

"Ned, I'm not *oppressing* you," said Father Albright with that spiritual expression that drives me up the wall. "We simply need the *room*. Terribly sorry."

Parolees? I could see the appeal, of course. Tried to regroup, but images of Father Albright as jailhouse counselor got in the way. Or was that *me* in the clerical collar rapping with a horny young ex-con? Did I miss my calling?

"So long as no one's *complained*," I repeated feebly.

"Take a month," he said. "Take two. Shall we say October 31st?"

What makes Episcopal priests so bloodless? Probably end up in a damp basement somewhere—GRO, I mean.

39. *Revenge*

KNOW THERE'S something fishy and don't even have my pants down before it comes out—not that Dr. Stern's the publisher's son *(that* I can figure out), but that he and Andrew had an affair!

"Meant nothing," Jay tells me. "I didn't even enjoy it."

Then we get down to business. There's a discharge to go with the burning, but that doesn't stop him from inspecting me more than strictly necessary. Swabs my urethra with a long Q-tip he dabs in a Petri dish. Latex hands are new to me. Whatever. I get a hard-on.

"Hmm," he says. "I'd say Andy's a lucky guy."

"Do you have a boyfriend?" I ask.

"Just split up," he says.

"Andrew had sex with you while you had a *boyfriend?"*

"Uh-huh: Denny."

That tramp! "Andrew and I love each other," I tell him. "We're faithful."

Gives a squeeze.

"Obviously," he says. "You're blushing."

"Until I met Andrew, I thought I was straight."

"Till *I* met him, thought I was gay."

He lets go, writes a prescription for tetracycline.

"And no sex for a week, you're contagious. Have you and Andy done it since your encounter?"

"Kind of."

"Send him along."

Get the prescription filled, then go to Andrew's new place—I have keys—to see what he has to say for himself. But he's not there.

Call Ned. "You never told me Andrew made it with Jay!"

"That was before *you* came along, I think."

"Well, I can't tell Andrew *he* treated me."

"Why not?"

"'Cause I'm so attracted to him. Ned, he's *handsome!"*

He laughs. *"Jay?"*

"And *smart*. He's a doctor!"

"Smart he is."

"How big is he?"

"How would I know? And why would you care?"

"I'm interested in such things, you know. Ned, I have more in common with *Jay* than with *Andrew!"*

"Cut it out, Edward! You and Andy are *deeply* involved—"

"So where *is* Andrew? Didn't say he was going out."

"Filling in for me at church."

"Awesome!"

"So you told him about your STD?"

"Yes."

"How'd he take it?"

"Gave me money for the doctor."

"He's a saint, Edward! How can you stand it?"

40. *Power Play*

I WAS WATCHING the 10:00 o'clock slaughter when Andy called on a staticky line from the street, *furious,* to tell me about *his* lurid evening: How, after lugging furniture all day, flattered I thought he might have learned anything worth passing on, he'd rushed off to church and, the 8:00 o'clock slot remaining open, and only one phone call coming in (from a young man who disclosed he was masturbating as they spoke), promptly fell asleep. Napped until Charlie's wide-open, avid young face came around the corner.

"Where's Ned?" Charlie asked.

"Sick," Andy replied. "I'm Andrew. Filling in, or trying to."

"I'm Charlie."

Delicious to look at, compact and sweet. Eyes a smear of blue, skin rosy, brown hair curly, nice hairy legs, shorts and T. And a very direct manner. Sixteen years old.

Charlie lounged on the couch—legs open, one sneaker parked on the desk—obviously troubled with an erection that wouldn't go away as he described how excited he got when someone tied him to a bedpost or came out with a belt.

Listening, falling into his eyes, Andy said he was aware of how quiet the building was, how resoundingly empty the church next door, and a moment later found himself standing locked in embrace with Charlie, lips grazing his curls and –

He stepped back.

"We can't do this, Charlie."

More amused than mad, Charlie was out the door a minute later. Sixteen going on 40.

Disillusioning. If his response to Edward's infidelity was going to be infidelity of his own, what kind of farce were they playing? That fucking Ned!

"I *resent* that," I told him. "By no means did I *plan* it. I'm ill, and frankly had enough respect for your maturity and self-control that I thought Charlie'd be safe with you. I was wrong, and I'm very disappointed. Sure, like any kid that age he's seductive as hell, wants to get a rise out of *everybody,* but to accuse me of setting you up with *jailbait* – "

"Did *you* have sex with Charlie?" he asked.

"I did not! Good Lord, Andy!"

No, turned me down flat. When, at our session, Charlie complained about wanting everything in pants, I blew smoke straight up into the air and held the pose, and with delightful scorn he said, "Not making it with *you,*" and that was that. Nothing more *I* could do for him.

"Andy, you're lashing out instead of realizing that what you did – *almost* did – with Charlie comes under the rubric of simple. . . Help me out here, what's the next word? Hello? *Hello!*"

"Revenge."

"Most natural thing in the world, and *sometimes* the most healing."

"We're supposed to be *faithful*—"

"*You* were faithful—until maybe a drag queen knocked on your door. Point is, you and Edward are back on an equal footing. Do you have any idea how *destructive* it is for a couple when one's guilty, the other forgiving? Talk about unstable! By some instinct I didn't know you possessed, this you have avoided.

"And do you think Edward would respect anything else you could do? In meeting his power play with one of your own, you did the only thing that could impress him. If you want to hold on to that boy—"

"I *do*, Ned, I *do*."

Did I hear sniffles? Pressed the telephone's little pair of horns.

Click.

"Andy, I've got another call. Bye-bye."

41. *L-O-S-E-R*

NED'S RIGHT ABOUT Jay and Andrew, of course. Scrub Andrew's new kitchen in an orgy of repentance. Still at it when he staggers in, poor tired baby.

Gives such a start when he sees me!

"Edward! Thought you were sleeping downtown! Don't you have work tomorrow?"

"So? This is closer."

"How was the doctor's?"

"Andrew, I know about you and Jay, and it's all right."

"Let's sit down," he goes. "Something I have to tell you."

"We're good here."

The *bastard!* Out of my sight two hours and grabs a *teenager?*

"Bastard! You were getting back at me."

"Revenge," he croaks, and here come the arms!

"'*Revenge,*'" I mock, and get him in the eye. Good one, too – bounces him off the wall.

"Get out!"

"I'm *getting* out" *etc. etc.*

I'm furious! At the One, jump the turnstile, clerk pretends not to see.

At least I have the asshole figured out: *symmetry*. If I sleep with ten guys, so will Andrew (or at least consider it, or at least *want* to): *Ten,* no more, no less. Could work him like a puppet if I wanted, but who wants to? Let him go to fucking *hell.*

Late when I get to East 10th. March upstairs, find the door ajar, push –

"Freeze!"

Holy shit! Guy in the kitchen pointing a *gun?*

Freeze? From pure shock I do a 360. But it must look sincere, he doesn't shoot. He's crouching by the airshaft, both hands on that thing. *Evil.*

Motions me in.

A voice says, "Don't you even have a fucking TV?"

I look, and on the couch is a cop with a beer on his knee, the cheap brand Andrew left a six-pack of.

"No," I go. "What's going on?"

Drains his can and ambles over. "You're Andrew Thomas?"

"No." Exchange of glances. Gun stays rock steady. "But I know him. Sublease from him."

They want I.D. Show my Library card. Things look bad. Cop grabs another beer, makes a quiet call on his radio.

"What's going on?" I ask Plainclothes.

Not a word. Keeps his piece on me. He's handsome, just doing his job. So I stand there contentedly as I can. Bathroom door's closed and water's tracked over the linoleum. Need to pee.

Cop speaks low to Plainclothes, who says, "OK, Eduardo, do us a favor?"

"Sure."

"He's going to open the door. Take a look, tell us who you see."

Never been so shaky. Both knees go *rat-a-tat-tat!* Cop belches without even trying not to and, eyes on me, swings open the bathroom door.

Light's on. The mirror over the sink is *smashed*. Tub's overflowing and in it, submerged, reposes Veronica in her red Angel Estrada. Water's trickling down a new hole in the floor by the toilet.

"Ceiling downstairs collapsed," cop says. "See, faucet runs. Not there," he adds, *shoving* me to the kitchen sink, where I throw up.

Plainclothes tucks his gun back in his sock. "Know her?"

"Yes," I say, temporarily losing it. "Yes, it's Pablo Escondido."

"*Pablo*?"

"Escondido."

They look at each other and, if you can believe it, the cop rolls up his sleeve, reaches in and feels her up, frees her dick to blossom like a flower. Veronica would have creamed.

The dress moves, reveals her knife at the bottom of the tub.

"The fucking size of that fucking thing!"

I go, "Where the fuck are the paramedics?"

"She's dead, don't worry. *He*. Care to tell us what happened?"

"What, like I did it?"

That they don't go for.

"Yeah, if that's what you did," cop goes.

"Citizen drowns in your bathtub—" says Plainclothes.

"She killed herself," I tell them.

Plain to me, Veronica crept like a cat out of Bellevue to die. Probably stole keys from Andrew. I'm betting on her treasured stash of sleeping pills like her god Marilyn Monroe, and that they hit her before she could cut her wrists.

"No note," goes Plainclothes.

"There's your note," I say, pointing to the mirror. "She hated her face."

But that's too deep for them.

"New one, breaking in to kill yourself."

"She lives upstairs," I say. "*Lived.* But she left her dresses here when she went in the hospital. She had AIDS, you know."

Do they hate me for that! Plainclothes takes two steps back, and the cop starts scrubbing his hands. Straight men are such pussies.

More cops arrive, one carrying a foul—*stinking!*—bodybag under his arm. Everybody takes a look, pulls a face. One says, "Thank God for the ceiling, didn't wait a week to call." That gives them a good laugh.

"OK, Eduardo," says Plainclothes while someone pulls the plug. Such an earnest sound, water going down the drain! "Going to the precinct, ask a few questions."

As seen on TV.

PROBABLY NOT A criminal matter, oinks the big dick at the station house. Just needs to know how a man ends up dead in my bathtub.

Woman, I correct him. Which leads to tension, but I owe it to her.

And can't help much. I mean, thanks a lot, Veronica, but if you're going to check out anyway whatever happened to jumping off the Empire State Building? And you wondered why you never made superstar?

Then the term *criminally negligent homicide* crops up. Negligent *what?* The *fuck* they talking about?

"Murder One," I snap. "I'll confess to nothing less. Why should I, for the perfect crime?"

At that I demand my phone call, and they're so irritated they hand me the whole phone.

Call Ned.

"Edward, it must be *3:00* in the morning!"

"I know, but I'm calling from the police station."

"What are you in for?"

"It's suicide, really, but–"

"*Suicide?* Don't tell me you're *that* stupid?"

"Not me, Pablo–"

"Why would they arrest *you?*"

Try to explain, but he's not tracking: "Edward, nothing I can do, I don't feel well, and I need my sleep." And having unloaded one two three, *bang!* in my ear.

So I do what I should have done in the first place, call Tia Luisa. Someone with *juice.*

"Be down right away, *muchacho,*" she tells me. "They beating on you?"

"No, Tia."

"Write down every badge number in sight, let them see you."

"Yes, Tia."

"*¡Bastardi!*" Still carrying on when we hang up.

Announce I'm getting sprung, would prefer to wait on the sidewalk and–get this!–they put me in the tank with the night's haul. They can't do that!

A crowded cage, one literally crappy toilet jutting out in the middle of junkies and muggers, and me in tears every time I pee. Only thing that saves me is when they ask what I'm in for, I say *homicide. Homicide* has *juice*. (I neglect to add *negligent*.)

Tia Luisa takes her sweet time, but finally I hear her arrive. "Where's my nephew? Where you put my dearest nephew?"

"Tia!" I shout. "Tia Luisa!"

She sails round the corner. Bless her, she's in full makeup and her hair is perfect!

"Eduardo, my poor— He's *locked up!* You locked up my nephew! Let him out! This instant!"

Which they do.

We have an emotional reunion. Pulls my head to her bosom and reads me the riot act about Veronica, devil in that one, only a matter of time *etc. etc.* Very polite to the cops, who are polite back, tell us they'll be in touch if the D.A. files charges.

Go out to her Town Car.

"Can I drop you?" she asks. Give her driver Andrew's address, it's on her way. "Your mother will *die*, Eduardo."

"Please don't tell Mami, Tia Luisa! She'd never get over it!"

"Such a handful. Everyone do so much for you, you take and take, never say, Time I pay back, what can I do for *you*."

"Owe you bigtime, Tia."

"You're a good boy, Eduardo. When you got your rest, call me."

Get out in front of Andrew's, wave goodbye, turn around and buzz. Watch yellow-gray light fill in between buildings across town, and buzz again.

On the speaker Andrew goes: "Who is it?"

"Me," in beaten mode.

Makes me wait, but the buzz comes.

I walk upstairs. He calls down, "Didn't think I'd see *you*

again." His eye's closed, *blooming,* red all around it, cheekbone purple.

"I did *that?* I'm sorry, Andrew. Forgive me?"

We stand against each other for a long time. When a door upstairs bangs and a brisk step starts downwards, he says, "Come in."

Tell him about Veronica and the cops. He can only shake his head.

"This city, it's too much," he goes. "Least it lets you know you're alive."

"Before it kills you."

"Don't see what they can do to you, though."

"They can't touch me," I declare. "When *I* kill someone, it's done *right.* Andrew, I don't want to break up. I love you, you know."

"Get some rest," he urges. "I need to think."

Gives me the bed. No sleep, though. Try, but the place is new, with new squeaks, new groans and Veronica enjoys haunting me. From time to time there comes a squeal like animals dying, which turns out to be bus drivers in the garage across the street stomping on their starters. Plus intimate clucks from pigeons dreaming on the windowsill.

Andrew sits up icing his eye all night. By the time I leave for work—he's taking the day off—it's a tropical blossom. A *beaut.*

At the door he says, "We'll have a long talk tonight?"

"Tonight? I really want a night in my own place at last."

"Well, then, call me." Manages a kiss.

WALK TO WORK like Frankenstein's monster, sleepwalk through my day. All I know is stick to routine. Last week of real money, school's starting up. Weather's still hot, but the heart's gone out of it. Soothing to take books out of the dumbwaiter, hand them out, get them back, send them down.

"You OK, Eddie?" Akesha asks. "You look funny."

"Never better."

Alan puts his hand on my shoulder, and he's not hitting on me, either.

"Eduardo, anything the matter?"

"Not a thing."

"Sure? Don't seem yourself."

"I'm *fine*, Alan, please stay out of my *face*."

That reassures him.

At lunch I call the Sixth Precinct to check on the status of my case.

"Nothing decided," they tell me.

Also call Ned—hitting Andrew, Veronica, the works.

Listens quietly, says, "You're right, the police will just wait till the higher-ups sign off. Andy's what's really on your mind. Here's a five-letter word to engrave on your heart, Edward: *L-o-s-e-r.*"

"Ned, I am *not*—"

"*Andy.* He's a *loser,* Edward. This is *not* going to work, unless by hitting him you woke him up, which I doubt: He's pretty dense."

Ned has a way of saying what you're thinking.

"Doesn't even fight back! Takes it just like my mom. You should see his eye!"

"Where are you staying?"

"East 10th, his old place."

"Is that a good idea?"

"Don't know where else— Hey, you mentioned a friend with room?"

"I *did?* Can't think who— Oh, that's right, my doctor friend, but I never checked—"

"*Jay?* What's his number?"

"No, no, Edward: He's so busy, working crazy hours and getting over that deplorable Denny."

"Ned."

"Let me sound him out first. Edward, if you have a minute, I refined my opening—"

"Not in the mood."

Does that stop him?

"Sounds like crap, Ned. Have to go."

42. *D.O.A.*

CALLED ANDY right away.

"Dump him, Andy. Edward told me all about it. Once someone hits you—"

"Ned, it's not good, but we can try to work it out."

"Aren't you getting a teensy bit tired of these reunions?"

Apparently I spoke heresy. He got huffy.

"I know the drill, Ned: One blow and it's over. But I'm not blameless in this. All night I kept replaying everything. Whose fault I almost did it with Charlie? Mine. Whose fault I have a job I loathe at *ORBS?* Mine. Whose fault I'm renting a place I can't really afford? Mine. And whose fault I haven't acted on my perception that by coming out I'm emotionally prepared to re-enter the classroom? *Mine!*

"So whose fault Edward hit me? Partly mine, in fact, and—"

"You *did* provoke him, Andy, and *deliberately,* because with his fist he completes your self-contempt."

"Nonsense! Where self-contempt enters the picture's because I'm trying to fit in where I don't belong, do work I don't care about, for reasons that shouldn't matter."

"It's not about *you,* Andy. The struggle to grow up when your father botched his job? Isn't even there? Edward needs someone far more mature than you, and you've no right— "

"Ned, you know what? None of your business."

"My friends *are* my business."

"Well, get this: Edward and I love each other."

"You don't think his attacking you hints at *ambivalence?* Andy, it's dangerous, and never right, to love someone who hits you. This is *not* going to work. Dump him, or he'll do it again. That's my last word on the subject.

"Now then: It's high time you moved into publishing— "

"I quit my job."

"You *what?"*

"Just now gave notice at *ORBS* and called Professor Onorato and got my old job back. Plus he's getting me into his doctoral program *and* a room as dorm advisor. Head in the right direction, it's downstream all the way."

"Andy, that's the stupidest thing I ever heard. That's your *future* you're throwing away! Had no idea you were this self-destructive!"

"Ned, you've done a lot for me and I'm grateful, but I think it's better that you don't call me again."

"Fine," I said, not trying to sound like anything but the old man I felt. *"Fine,* Andy. Good luck."

I hung up, affronted. *Killed* Plan *"A."* Plan *"A"* for *Andy*? D.O.A.

Returned to my manuscript, inserting a comma and dancing a semi-colon around. But I was just fiddling.

43. *Macy's*

REASSURING AFTERNOON of pneumatic clicks and whining cables. Then it's time to go home, to my own place at last! Hope the hole by the toilet's plugged, but whatever.

Get fancy and take the R. Never pays, taking a train you don't know. Takes forever. Rolling into Madison Square there's a bump, and everybody looks at each other hoping we ran over someone. Doors open and stay open, conductor goes, "Friends and customers, what can I say?" People dash down the stairs, can't believe their luck, pile on board triumphant, then wait and wait. But somehow Veronica's death gives me patience.

Finally get to East 10th. Wind up the stairs, keys out, get to my door and—*padlocked*. Padlocked latches are bolted to door and frame. Unlocking the deadbolts does nothing.

Beat on Mrs. Economides' door. "Fuck they do to my door?"

"Illegal tenant," she screeches through steel. "Sublease without permission!"

"Shit! My stuff's in there!"

Cackles for pure joy. "Look in the trash."

"Excuse me?" Kick till she mentions police, then go out to the garbage cans. A reeking homeless guy sitting on Andrew's couch is holding up my spare Wranglers with a critical eye.

"Go fuck yourself," I suggest, and collect what's left. Tell the truth, all I care about are my books for school, and they're there.

Lug everything uptown—on the good old One this time—and buzz Andrew.

"Who is it?"

"Me."

The buzz comes, I trudge upstairs.

"Thought you were staying downtown tonight?"

Set down my worldly goods. "Get this, they took my apartment. *Your* apartment."

"What?"

"Padlocked it."

"Can they *do* that?"

"Andrew, they can do anything they want," I inform him.

"What about your stuff?"

"Threw it out, can you believe it? But you lost your couch and bed."

"No loss. At least we can have our talk."

Slap his hand off like it's a mosquito. "Listen, can it wait? I'm dead on my feet. *Please,* Andrew?"

"I gave notice at *ORBS* today – "

"Why?"

" – after scoring tetracycline from the company doctor, and got my Terse job back. I'm going back to school."

"No shit! Cool! Hey, I wanted that Terse job!"

"To burrow, burrow, burrow, chip, chip, chip, gnaw, gnaw, gnaw?"

"You're so funny," I say.

Fixes dinner, and we make it an early night.

"I can't *sleep* with you, Andrew. You know what would happen."

"True."

"Floor's fine."

We make a nest of sheets and blankets for me, cozy enough, and Andrew climbs the loft.

"You OK down there?"

"This is great," I go. "Like camping out."

"You've gone camping?"

"*Yes*. Fresh Air Fund when I was ten."

"Let me know if it gets too hard and we'll switch."

"If *what* gets too hard?"

"The floor, you pervert."

Exchange long distance *love you's* and sleep like the dead.

IN THE MORNING Andrew says first thing, "We need to talk, Edward."

Talk, talk; sure, sure. "Tonight?"

"Hold you to it. How's my eye? Better?"

"Wait, there's a yellow rim. That's a sign of healing."

Looks in the mirror. "It's worse! It's *neon!*"

"Sorry."

Soon after the Library opens, Jaime comes up to the cage, hands me an envelope, says, *"Tia Luisa dice que la llame."*

Open it when I have a chance. It's about what I expect: a list folded around a platinum American Express card complete with hologram. Beautiful! The list is something else: Donna Karan handbags, scarves, belts, boots, jackets, that sort of thing—small but pricey. Not too flattered that Tia Luisa thinks I'll look natural buying women's stuff, though.

Call her at lunch.

"Saved my life the other night, Tia."

"You're precious to me, Eduardo, like my own son. Jaime come by?"

"Yes, Tia."

"Catch up on your rest?"

"Yes, thank you, Tia."

"How late you work today?"

"Till 6:00."

"You're a hardworking boy, 6:00 is perfect. What Jaime gave you? Guaranteed good. See the shopping list?"

"Yes, Tia."

"Go to Macy's DKNY boutique, check off that list, we're good, OK?"

"OK."

"Macy's open late tonight, so don't rush. You got your own life to live, I won't bother you again."

"It's no bother, Tia."

"But tell me if you like it. Jaime say where to take it?"

"Yes, Tia, I'm all set."

"Good. And Eduardo?"

"Yes?"

"Get something special for your Mami. Winter coming before you know. Get her a coat. What that woman goes through!"

"With me for a son, what do you expect?"

"So go a little crazy for her. Something *nice*. But DKNY."

"Thank you, Tia. I love you."

"Love *you*, Eduardo. Have fun."

Nothing to do but get it over. As I'm leaving, Akesha goes, "Get a bite, Eddie?"

"Can't, got shopping."

Macy's is ten minutes from the Library. I love Macy's. Everything looks so good in there, feel rich just looking.

Take a deep breath going in, look cool, find DKNY upstairs and start picking out stuff—choosily, like I'm trying to make up my mind. This clerk comes up to help. Plump, well groomed, with the moist, pink skin, every hair fluffed and in place, fingertips wired to the *Bright* control on his eyes, where commissions start dancing. Gets off rubbing the leathers and silks.

"You're shopping for—?"

"My mom. Dad gave me a list."

"I can see you're a man of taste."

Time for Mami's coat. Find a terrific mid-length in butter-soft leather marked down to $499 and know she'll love it. But don't know what color she likes. Usually she wears brown, sometimes old-lady black, but I'm not sure if this is her taste or her penance, so I hesitate between brown and red-purple. Decide on brown, to be safe.

My guy wraps everything in tissue with the dexterity of a priest at the altar. So turned on! Always wondered why people work retail, and that must be the answer: *Sex,* the everything answer. Discreetly creams, folding Mami's coat. Boxes the scarves and gloves, stows everything in four shopping bags. His smile as I hand over the platinum shows no loss of confidence, though he pays attention to what he's doing. I sign for $3,219.48 worth of stuff. Signature's close enough, right? Can't practice these things, I can't, anyway.

Everything goes through, he wishes me a good evening and points out the elevator. Pick up my bags, say the escalator's fine, slide downstairs and leisurely take the long way out to Seventh Avenue, stopping to get interested in polo shirts along the way. Remember to keep up my station by waiting for a taxi. I admit, breathe easier once I'm in it.

Give the address, 47th off Second, where I leave the stuff and the platinum. Then walk the bag with Mami's coat over to Grand Central, catch the shuttle to Times Square, trundle uptown on the One.

Now I'm feeling happy. My homecoming.

THEY'RE WATCHING TV when I come through the door—the old 19-inch, which gives me a pang. Ramrod straight, José has place of honor in the middle of the couch, legs spread, Mami angled away from him on the slippery plastic, Joselito on a chair off the other side.

Mami's so happy to see me, taps my cheek, even, and she's

not a toucher. No warm folds of maternal flesh for me *etc. etc.* which in the long run's better. The others hold in their joy at seeing me.

They want to know about Veronica, but what can I say? Tell me her funeral's waiting on the City to release the body, and will take place at a parlor in Inwood. She would *die.* If not Campbell's, where they buried Judy Garland from, why not some place downtown where her buds can go without getting killed? But no, she'll be laid out uptown in her father's oldest suit. Say I'll give it a miss.

Mami says something to José about *it,* and José sends Joselito to the kitchen to get *it* from on top of the fridge, he hands *it* to José, who gives *it* to Mami, who hands *it* to me. It's a letter to me from the City, already opened, saying a public assistance client's named me as the father on her infant's birth certificate and demanding I pay child support or state cause why not, *i.e.,* get a paternity test.

"What's this shit?" I ask with mixed emotions. "She *had* it?"

José & Son concentrate on their TV gunfire as Mami says, *"Bebé, cinco libras y seis onzas."*

"Scrawny!" I go, but she has to see the pride in my eyes. Tells me Suriya's moved back in upstairs. Ask what happened to her mother, and hear she got Albion, 7-to-10.

Poor Suriya, joining the families lined up at Columbus Circle Friday nights for the overnight bus.

Mami says there's more mail for me on top of her dresser. Get it myself, a blue envelope excessively stamped with Fidel's beard, return address Havana. Carry it to the living room and tear it open. Mami looks over very sly:

> My dear son Eduardo,
> Your letter made my heart leap with great joy *etc. etc.*

Give it to Mami, see her heart leaping with great joy.

Moment's ripe. Push the Macy's bag at her.

"Mami, this is for you. Late birthday."

She's astonished. Takes out the coat, is *stunned!* Thrilled! Hit of the century! Puts it on, kisses me, says over and over how much she loves it.

"José, *¡mira!*" Models it, hands fluttering over the leather, hardly daring to touch it. "*¡Mira!*"

José swivels his head for a big half-second.

"Shit color."

Her face falls.

"I'll take it back," I tell her. "What color's good?"

Turns out red-purple's *perfect*. Kisses me as I leave, and slips my father's letter in my pocket.

GO TO ANDREW'S. Looks at the Macy's bag and goes, "For me?"

"For my Mom."

"That's great, Edward. Look, let's sit down, have our talk."

"So talk already!" Hand him my letters.

"What are *these?*"

"Which one's that—City's? Says I made a girl pregnant last winter, like."

"Did you?"

"Could be."

"Can they make you—?"

"What, I should abandon my son? But I'm going for the paternity test first thing." Look at it. "Twenty-Seventh Street? Before work."

"If it's yours, what—?"

"Quit school, support the brat."

He studies the bearded envelope. "And this?"

"First thing my father ever gave me."

"Your *father?* May I?" Takes out the letter, gathers my father's joy at hearing from me, to whom, incidentally, he has by his *wife* given two half-sisters and a half-brother.

"Edward, this is *wonderful!*" he goes, and pushes a kitchen chair at me. "Look, I've been thinking. Let's go back to the beginning. I seduced you, so from the start—"

"You never seduced me, I *wanted* to. Andrew, I'll never, *never* hit you again."

"Just so you know that for me paradise lies in you."

"No wonder white people love *love*, you've got it down to real estate!"

Comes out flip, but suddenly I'm crying. *Weeping*. A *river!* A fucking *Mississippi!* I'd shake apart if Andrew didn't grab me like a boa constrictor!

"There, there," he goes. "There, there."

"Fuck fuck fuck fuck *fuck!* If only I accepted I was gay years ago— Couldn't even do *that*— Now I've fucked up *everything!* Fucked up my *life,* Andrew!"

Encases me in *cement.* "No, you haven't, Edward. You have me, I'm right here with you, we'll work it out together." As I finally calm down and stop heaving, he says, "I don't make it easy for you."

"Say that again!"

"It's taken me 27 years to find you. Didn't find you maybe where I expected, but that you're what I want—*you, Edward*—I have no doubt. I love you, and know with work on both sides, we can get back to—better than ever, and stay that way as long as we want." The arms squeeze! "What do you think? Can we kiss? Or would that cross-infect us?"

"Who cares?"

We kiss, we jump on each other, we exhaust ourselves with each other, then *bang!* we're asleep.

DEEP SLEEP, but not enough. Hot shower, no breakfast, *run*—soon as I can slip out of Andrew's *hug*—down to Ninth Avenue and 27th Street, Macy's bag in hand. There the mournfullest trees in town—leaves already going yellow—hide where the City treats such STDs as male fertility.

Wave my letter at the nurse at the door. "Where do I go—?"

"Downstairs."

Place looks like a school, covered with tile so pitted and gray there's no gleam left. And stinks! Knock at a shaky door, *Paternity* painted on frosted glass. No response. Stick my head in. A nurse behind the desk swallows a mouthful of bagel.

"Paternity?" she goes. "Fill this out."

Her pinky puts me in a chair at the wall. Through the opening behind her are lab tables, microscopes, beakers and tubes filled with gunk, a few city employees moving slow. I can't look.

Put down my stats and the case number, sign a statement beneath a big fat *If*, give it back, and suddenly she's a ribald old number.

"Knocked her up, did we?"

"Maybe."

"We'll just see."

"What do you do?"

"Take blood from your finger and type it under the scope," she says. "Check it's consistent with baby's. Let's see, baby's type O and Mom's O, so *you* better be O."

Swabs my finger, takes it to her bosom, bares her teeth, pricks.

"Ouch!"

"Big man," she says with pleasure, pinching up a drop and touching a slide to it. "This is way easier than DNA, but say you *are* O, that's the commonest, have to go to DNA, be *sure*. Wait if you want, or—"

"I'll wait."

Rings a bell, hunts down another bagel. Eventually a West Indian-looking lady technician picks up the slide, takes it to a lab table. Time passes. A few scared-looking losers trail in, fill out their forms.

Finally the West Indian woman returns with a card.

"OK, Eduardo, moment of truth," says the nurse, reaching. "Let's see—*Ohh!*" My heart goes through the floor! "No way that's your baby: *You're* AB. Poor little thing."

"Thank you, God!" Slap five all around. She is not pleased. Takes time finishing my form of absolution. I kiss it.

But have to postpone celebrating until after Macy's if I want to get to work any time soon. Shift starts at 10:00, same time Macy's opens, but 20 minutes late I can swing, no sweat. Enter on Seventh Avenue as they unlock the doors, but have to go all the way to the Broadway desk to ask where to exchange the coat.

"Refund or exchange?"

"Exchange."

"Just take it up to the Donna Karan boutique."

Take the escalator through rising mists of perfume. See *Gift Wrapping* on the balcony, kick myself for not thinking. Then sail up to DKNY.

"Hi," I go, bringing out the coat. "Got this for my mom, but she wants a different color. Lost the sales slip, but the tags are still on."

"No problem," says the clerk. She scans a tag and hits a key. "One moment."

And a dick waddles up! Obvious as hell, gut spreading his blazer!

"This him?" he goes. "OK, sir, come with me."

"They said exchange it here, I don't want a *refund*."

"This way," he says without inflection.

"The *fuck* is going on? Just exchanging a *coat* for my *mother!*"

Put on a show, but it doesn't do any good. Don't run, I've seen it tried—half the "shoppers" in that dump are dicks in disguise. Locks me in a room with a barred door.

"Hey, I know my rights!" I yell as he walks away, adding sarcastically, *"Sir?"*

"Police'll be here soon," he says like he's going out of his way to be host-like.

All along, I know there's a chance of what's happening happening, but I thought only a small one. Frankly had more faith in Tia Luisa than that.

Two cops arrive and arrest me, cuff me, remember (fuck it!) to read me my rights, walk me outdoors like a Ten Most Wanted, drive me two blocks to Midtown South. There they park me on a bench while they and their buddies recite every sports score in history and eat their crummy pizza without sharing.

Though they do perk up at *negligent homicide.*

"Excuse me?" I finally have to hint. "Think I get a phone call?"

Call Tia Luisa, naturally.

"Some kind of record for *stupid,"* she says.

"I know, Tia, I'm sorry."

"Something fall off the truck, give thanks to *God,* don't ask, 'It come in my color?'"

"You're right, Tia."

"Going to get serious bail, don't know why I should bother."

"Me neither, Tia."

"Have to work your tail off, and that's *if* you could stop being stupid, which I have my doubts."

"I know, Tia, so do I. I'm sorry." My voice is as humble as it gets.

"And me still trying to get your *maricón* friend out of the City, which cut him up like a piece of meat." With new crispness, she says, "I'll let your Mami know, all I can do. My name come up, be very sad. And Eduardo?"

"Yes, Tia Luisa?"

"They take you to Central Booking, you watch your ass."

And hangs up! Reads me upside down, inside out and hangs up on *me*, her favorite godson!

44. *Cancer Redux*

DAWN AWAKENED ME with pure inspiration—a morning such as I never thought to see again!

Called Andy to get his take.

"Excuse me, Ned? Didn't I say not to call me?"

"Oh, you meant it? Two minutes, Andy—and your honest opinion, remember, though I *think* I was taking dictation from God." Cleared my throat as he hung on. Can't beat that early training in manners. Read my new opening paragraph, and paused. "Well?"

"This book's your masturbation fantasy, right?"

I was speechless! Though not literally so.

"*Masturbation* fantasy? Andy, I'm telling a story of *shame,* melding literal levels to underlying metaphor—"

"OK, it's a masterpiece," he said. "Ned, I can't see it any more. And please pay me the respect to take me seriously when I say—"

Click. Thank God.

"Hold on, Andy." *Click*. "Hello?"

From the bottom of a well: "Ned, I'm in jail. I need bail money."

"Who'd you kill this time?"

"Not funny. Charging me with felony grand larceny third degree."

"What'd you do?"

"Shoplifted a coat for my Mom, but she wanted a different color, so I took it back and – "

"Paging Dr. Freud," I said. "Obviously you *wanted* to get caught, so be glad you *were*. Edward, I'm on the phone. I suggest you let Andy know – "

"Line's busy and he doesn't have call waiting, thinks it's *rude*."

"Keep trying, though I doubt he's got *bail* money. How much is it?"

"Not set, but they say probably a thousand in cash will do it."

Sounded so miserable, I took pity on him. "You don't want to go back there, anyway. Tell you what, let me call Jay right now, see if he'll put you up."

"*Would* you?"

"But how do I let you know?"

"Call my mom?" Gave me her number. "Thing is, Ned, she doesn't speak English, so just say *'Por Eduardo* – '"

"I like that: 'Poor Eduardo.'"

" – and Jay's number. She's good at numbers."

"Have to go." *Click*. "Where were we, Andy?"

"Ned, why can't you leave Edward and me to figure things out ourselves?"

"Andy, I've tried – God knows I've *tried* – to help you find a balance of power, but – Tell me, *who* in your relationship has more power, you or Edward?"

"Dammit, Ned, *you* do. Why am I fighting for the love of my life talking to *you?"*

"Because you haven't really accepted your sexuality—"

"What!"

"—as shown by your return to the wars of the footnotes."

"You have it ass-backwards, Ned. I don't know what your plan is—"

"I have no plan, and the only *power* I have over anyone is what he gives me. And let me tell you: If you don't *use* power, you don't *have* it.

"Andy, I'm an artist. Sorry if that means my character's deficient, but nobody ever said Picasso was a nice guy. *Warhol* even worse! Who *cares* how nasty he was? Put in his stint every day, the rest fed the work, the work remains and that's enough for me."

"You're no artist," he said. "You're a bitter, aging, ineffective—"

"Can't you hear the homophobia? Whether you accept it or not, it's *over,* Andy, and it's *Edward* we have to worry about."

"Ned, he lacks self-esteem, but he's not so damaged that we can't—"

"Can't imagine what he'll do. Become a writer? At least if he does time he'll come out with material, and prison stories *always* make a hit. Must be middle-class guilt."

"They won't charge him, autopsy's sure to turn up barbiturates—"

"Don't you know?"

"Know *what?"*

"Edward's in stir as we speak. Shoplifting, is it?"

"Fuck! Fuck fuck *fuck!* Know what you are, Ned? A fucking *virus*. What's the point when after the virus kills the host, it dies, too?"

Couldn't resist. "Self-expression?"

"Goodbye, *asshole*."

"And fuck you, too," I said, and hung up. Pulled Dolly's ears. "*Kids* today, old boy. What's the world *coming* to? But my sixth sense tells me that Edward's going to see us into print."

Opened my address book and put a diagonal through Andy's name. Phoned Jay, learned he'd be happy to host Edward. Calling Edward's mom, I retrieved enough Spanish from my year on Majorca to dictate Jay's number.

Then I peed and washed my hands and face. Why was it time to study my reflection? The dying actor always looks deepest into the camera; surely not *that?*

The mirror showed that face in all Creation I'm most tired of, but behind one well-formed nostril I espied something new, an angry black extrusion, a crinkle of bubbling boiled pitch.

Called Dr. Kushner's office to announce I'd be there in half an hour with an emergency.

45. *Graduation Photo*

PUT ME IN a lineup. *Cool!* March five of us out, give commands from behind a mirror. I admire how innocent I look. Do our turns on cue, mine dedicated to Veronica. Three of us are Latino, but for sure one's a cop. Whoever hires cops in New York goes for the sexy young guys with kissable lips. (If you ask me, what happens to them after a year on the force is a crime.)

Walk me back to the tank. Through a doorway I see the Macy's clerk from last night. Looks excited, licking his lips and wearing glasses he didn't have on in the store.

Feel better, though they bus me downtown and book me anyway. Give me a lawyer, take me into a courtroom for arraignment. *Cool!*

Thank God the judge is a Black woman! My lawyer tells how the myopic Macy's clerk thought the lineup was *The Dating Game,* chose contestant number three – the cop – no jury in the land would convict. Judge asks what I have to say, and I tell her about being a young Latino in NYC, you're walking down the street or shopping and cops handcuff you, I work at the Public Library, honors student at City College *etc. etc.*

She enjoys it, but turns mean after the assistant D.A.'s gobbledygook about card reported stolen, organized ring, caught red-handed *etc. etc.*

Sets bail: I need to come up with $1,000 in cash. My lawyer suggests a plea, but I tell him he's crazy. Bite the bullet and call Mami.

What a weeper. Tia Luisa's already told her the college son's in jail, so she has an inkling her coat might be out the window, but a *thousand dollars!* Even the cops look embarrassed.

Into the cells I go. Take the toilet paper out of the hands of a guy – "I need that" – and using spit and my pinky write a letter to my father. Naturally as it dries it vanishes.

Finally somebody shouts, "*Que*-sada!"

Shout back, "*De* Quesada?"

They release me and give me back my belt and shoelaces. Ask for Mami's coat, too, but they're so peeved I don't insist.

Ivan the numbers collector is waiting.

"Ivan! *¡Gracias!*"

"*De nada,*" he goes with a hideous – *grin* comes closest. One eye says one thing, the glass one another.

Andrew blunders in just in time to recoil from Ivan like he's Boris Karloff.

"Edward! Ned told me–"

"Hey, be cool."

"You're out!"

"Natch. You look wan. Ivan, *¡gracias de nuevo!"*

We take the One to Andrew's.

"Starving," I complain.

"Order in? Ralph's?"

Green pepper and sausage pizza arrives as I step out of the shower.

"Take your tetracycline?" Andrew asks.

"Don't worry about it. *Yes.* Never been so *tired,"* I complain, stuffing my face.

"We'll get you right to bed."

"Can't stay. My mom wants to see me."

"Of course. Can I come up and meet her? Please?"

"If you want."

Write my letter before I forget, ask for an envelope and enough stamps for a letter to Cuba, and he asks who I'm writing to.

"Were you always this nosy? Here."

> August 25, 1991
>
> My father,
>
> Why do you abandon me? Why do you not legitimate me? Why do you force your eldest son to make his way through life alone?
>
> Your son,
> Eduardo de Quesada

"Edward, you can't send this! This cuts off relations forever!"

"Good."

"He may be a bad father, but he's *yours.*"

"Who needs him? *Ned's* more my father."

"Ned's a *false* father, an *evil*– "

"Ned helped *you* grow up, why can't he help me? Come on if you're coming."

"Edward– "

Arms reach around me, but I wriggle free. *"Don't,* Mami's worried."

We walk to 59th for the One. A woman, expression set, passes carrying a stuffed lamb as I drop my letter in a mailbox. Flap the lid extra times to be *sure.*

On the train Andrew remembers: "What happened with your blood test?"

People look.

I go, "Louder, please. Not mine."

"That's great! Thank goodness!"

Run off the train at 137th Street. Hear him scrambling after, across Broadway, up and around the corner, into the lobby, where *compadres* hanging out, paper bags in hand, high-five me. "Visiting the Old Country, *¿muchacho?"* one asks. Another sees Andrew's eye and lands his fist in his palm: *"Pow!"*

Take the stairs two at a time, step into a burst of happy Spanish. Andrew trails in behind as I'm disengaging from Mami and turning to Suriya, who holds the tiny baby who bears my name. On the couch José presides like a deity.

Touch Eduardo, Jr.'s cheek. Squatting, gently take him in my arms. Stand up kissing him. Everybody watches indulgently.

Sneering from a chair, Joselito asks about my shadow.

"Mi amigo Andrew."

Andrew closes the door and formally shakes hands with everybody. Mami asks him what he wants to drink, sends Joselito to the kitchen for Pepsi, goes into her cleavage for Jay's number, hands it to me.

Kiss the child again. It doesn't mind a bit.

"She brought it by to introduce," I tell Andrew, holding out a tiny arm. "Wave to Uncle Andrew."

"Never seen you so *radiant,*" he sees fit to announce.

Eduardo, Jr. messes his diaper, and the women whisk him away while I carry the phone around the corner and fix things with Jay.

When I come back Andrew quietly asks, "Did you tell her?"

"Tell her *what?*"

"About the blood test?"

José's head snaps towards us. Smiles at Andrew, Andrew beams back. The mothers return, I kiss them and the baby, everybody goes, *"Oooh."*

"Can I talk to you?" I say, and go out to the hallway. Shaking hands all around, Andrew's out the door behind me. I go, "How could you *say* that? In front of everybody?"

"What do you mean?"

"Andrew, who's going to take care of him if I don't? *Welfare?*"

"But Edward– "

"And when will *I* ever have a son if not now?"

"But– "

"I don't want your *honey*. Ned's right about you: You're a *loser!*"

"I'm a loser?"

That's it. Get him square on the chin.

"Go to fucking hell, *cocksucker!*"

Staggers downstairs. Stand by the window, kneading my fist. Moment of peace; not many in this life. Laughter as he goes through the lobby. As he comes out to the sidewalk see him tasting blood. See him thinking, *Go to hell? Can't be far.*

Decides to walk it. Sets off down Broadway, past the bodegas, botanicas and auto-repair shops. Soon he'll cross 125, climb towards Columbia's campus—blocky and formal, ways cleared for artillery to keep the kids in line—and see pretty young guys tossing Frisbees as darkness swallows them up. Maybe one will smile and go, *"Catch!"*

Feeling his chin, hoping nightfall will keep people from noticing his eye, he'll watch the moon as it gets a shine rising through the murk. No place in New York's dark enough, everybody stares, but he'll figure his broken chin and black eye are badges of a queer's progress.

Downtown he'll see the Empire State Building, its top red and blue but stony and austere beneath the colors. On its observation deck flashbulbs will pop tiny pinpricks of light. Such optimism to think your flash will bleach Manhattan, reveal it posing for you. But flashbulbs pop steadily from on high every night.

He'll smile up at them—say *Cheese* for his graduation photo—and go home.

Meanwhile I return to my son.